Peter King Salter

**Whitepatch**

A romance for quiet people. Part 2

Peter King Salter

**Whitepatch**
*A romance for quiet people. Part 2*

ISBN/EAN: 9783337052331

Printed in Europe, USA, Canada, Australia, Japan

Cover: Foto ©Andreas Hilbeck / pixelio.de

More available books at **www.hansebooks.com**

# WHITEPATCH.

## A ROMANCE FOR QUIET PEOPLE.

"Il faudrait avoir le courage de ne se préoccuper ni des succès du salon ni de l'opinion de la presse, ni de l'éventualité des récompenses, et ne s'inquiéter que de se contenter soi-même."—ALFRED STEPHENS, *Impressions sur la Peinture.*

"Wholesomeness is the salt of life."—*Spanish Proverb.*

## IN THREE VOLUMES.

## VOL. II.

## LONDON:

RICHARD BENTLEY AND SON,

Publishers in Ordinary to Her Majesty the Queen.

1887.

# CONTENTS OF VOL. II.

# WHITEPATCH.

## CHAPTER I.

### THE GHOST OF THE GARDEN.

A FEW mornings after these events Mary was very busy in her room carving a lovely tombstone for Mr. Grego's grave in the little garden, in real white marble, inscribing, with deep-cut fanciful letters, to be afterwards filled in with gold, vermilion, and other colours, his many amiable qualities and high talents, and his tragic end—giving his age as one hundred and twenty, which Harrison had said she might do with certainty; and, as a text at the bottom, which would recall him to the affectionate remembrance of friends and admirers, his great performance, " Turn the hands out! shorten sail!"

The king was decidedly better, though still confined to Mary's bedroom, and Harrison thought he would pull through. Solomon, though he could never take the place of Mr. Grego, was nevertheless a very amusing bird, producing old English proverbs and scraps of poetry at absurd moments, and quickly learning to imitate Spillett's voice. Although the sad look would still often return to Mary's eyes, youth and nature were asserting their rights, and she was on the whole more cheerful and like herself, when Spillett came up with two pieces of news—the ghost in the garden, which no one living had ever seen, had at last appeared; and

a very tall strange gentleman had come
to stay at the Little Sack. Mary first
coloured violently, then turned very white,
and her hand trembled as she went on with
her carving. Spillett ran on about the
new apparition, which she had before
believed to be almost entirely her own
invention.

"There is no doubt about it, ma'am.
William" (the under groom, who slept in
the house) "saw it distinctly as he was
coming in to prayers the night before last,
standing as if it had been a tree in the
ground in the kitchen-garden—by the wall
just there under your windows, Miss Mary;
and Mr. Mungham" (the cowman) "last
Monday night saw it go through the
cherry orchard and disappear like a flash.
He was quite sure of it—there wasn't any
human being born as tall as that, and

William says the same; it stood up higher than the wall, and it was so still he didn't know at the time what it was. He thought it was something the gardeners had planted there."

Poor Mary listened with her head bent down and her heart beating rapidly.

" Oh, nonsense, Spillett," she murmured; " they must have fancied it."

" No, indeed, Miss Mary! they are quite sure, and Mrs. Walker looks awfully pale since she heard of it. But she hasn't said anything more about going since that night she went to the old dairy; but she's as bad as ever to the maids, and Eliza says she shall go if she stops, it is quite impossible to please her—what's right one day is wrong the next. Eliza is so bothered that she boiled a duck yesterday instead of a fowl; and then Mrs. Walker said she was worse than a landlubber in a ship's galley. What's a landlubber, Miss Mary? Eliza says she is sure it is something dreadfully low, like ' scum of the earth.' "

" Landlubber, Spillett—I am not quite sure exactly ; you had better ask Harrison. I know a ship's galley is the place where they cook."

" So I did, ma'am ; but he laughed and said it was the scullery-maid on board ship.  But I never heard they kept maids on board ship, and I don't believe it's that."

" We had better look in Dr. Johnson," said Mary.

" And Mr. Harrison lost his temper yesterday, and told Mrs. Walker to go to the devil about the Colonel's cheese—that's sure to go straight to Miss Doddingstead ; and father's furious, too, as she has been

interfering and changing the time of the
men coming in to supper, and father was
a little hot with her, and she told him
to go and rake up his stable-muck, and
not be dictating to her—that to father!—
and it will be a miracle if there is any
one of us here, except Mrs. Jenkins, by
Christmas-time."

Mary, notwithstanding her agitation,
was moved by the prospect of this dreadful
revolution, and she endeavoured to cheer
Spillett by saying that, " she did not think
her grandfather would really support Mrs.
Walker when he knew all, as she had
heard him say to her aunt one morning
after prayers, when Mrs. Walker first
came, that she 'looked like an old
harridan.' "

Spillett said " she hoped it might be so,
but the Colonel was so obstinate that you

could never count upon anything with him except the contrary."

"But who can the strange gentleman at the Little Sack be, Spillett?" said Mary, unable to bear any longer in silence the weight of her thoughts.

"Whoop! *Naughty* bird!" cried Solomon.

Mary became very red again, made a slip with her chisel, and spoilt a letter.

Spillett, brought back from her own affairs, thought a moment, and then she exclaimed, "I shouldn't wonder if it's him, Miss Mary!"

"How *very* wrong and imprudent," said Mary, though half an hour before she had been thinking of what she would have done if she had been a man. She had written to her friend the Hon. Dick, as he requested, and had not been quite pleased

at hearing nothing from him in return.
"If grandpapa should hear of it! But
I shall not go outside the garden, Spillett,
until I hear he is gone."

"But it might not be him after all, Miss
Mary. Captain Huntingcroft may have
lent it to some one else."

This idea, however, did not seem to
please Mary either; and she went on
carving in silence.

"No one has heard his name, ma'am,
and you might as well try to get an
answer out of a sign-post as Mrs. Crippin,
who takes care now of the Little Sack.
But they say he doesn't shoot or hunt, and
walks about by himself all day in the side
lanes and places."

Mary's heart beat rapidly again.

"I think I shall go down in the garden
and look at the queen, Spillett."

She put down her tools, and went to her room to get her hat, and Spillett remained cogitating over many matters as she sat at work near the window.

"It is a long lane that has no turning," said Solomon, catching the word "lane," and he went on whooping and quoting Hamlet, till Spillett, getting impatient, rose and covered him with a cloth.

That evening Ruth the scullery-maid was engaged in the unpoetic business of washing dishes in the strange old back kitchen of the Manor-house. And yet the scene had a certain poetry of its own, for Ruth was a very pretty girl, clean and neat in her dress, notwithstanding her occupation, and the quaint old place, that looked as if it had long passed from human care except for an occasional rough coat of whitewash in the summer, was full of association with for-

gotten generations. Its great copper boiler
in the corner, that had cooked food for end-
less successions of birds and animals, now of
the same dust as their masters, was out of
date and as green as an old brass cannon;
the huge grate that once glowed with broad
fires which roasted monster joints in the
press of busy feasts of old, was now silent
and dark with slow rust, and its wide
mantelpiece, broad and heavy as a seat by
the wayside—with its pewter plates and
tall pewter candlesticks grey with age and
long neglect was mournful as a flower-
garden in autumn. Round the walls strong
shelves, bent and inclining, yet still holding
gigantic pots, kettles, and pans of a past
time—once bright and the pride of the
kitchen, now despised and uncared for—
were humble examples of departed great-
ness. Overhead the deep beams in the

ceiling had sunk here and there, and the uncouth iron hooks bedded in the hardened oak were now rusted and un- profitable. Against the side the antique wooden dresser was bare and unfurnished, and had long been deserted for its younger rival in the kitchen—itself an antiquity despised by Mrs. Walker; the fantastic old pump, tall and solemn as a grenadier, yet comical as a clown with its odd spout and long curved handle, was a homely con- temporary of the lordly Don Carlos; and the dark old window with its iron bars, that never knew blind or curtain, resembled that of an old prison or convent. All this, lighted by one small modern candle that gave shapes and shadows like the goblin forms of a departed age, contrasted strongly with the blooming Ruth, her round bare arms, and her neat dress pinned up behind

her, finishing her task with a cheerful
seriousness that was happiness in the
peaceful and solitary obscurity. But such
continuous and exciting sounds of laughter
now came from the distance, that Ruth,
hastily wiping her hands on her apron, ran
off to see what it was all about, and found
John entertaining the maids by an imitation
of the common enemy, Mrs. Walker.

This ill-used and much misunderstood
person was making her round of nightly
inspection before prayers; and coming in
by a side door to the back kitchen, she found
the candle burning and Ruth absent, with
her work unfinished. She was of opinion
that Ruth was much too good-looking a girl
to be in a gentleman's house, as the men
were always stopping her in the passages;
and she had settled in her mind to recom-
mend Miss Doddingstead to change her for

a more matter-of-fact Cinderella. She even suspected her of going out after dark " gallivanting " with the stable men—a matter of which the girl was entirely innocent ; so she opened the back door and went out into the kitchen court. This place was almost a garden, with a grass plot having a cherry tree in the centre. The building, with broad brick pavements, ran round three sides, and the fourth was separated from the kitchen-garden by high trellis-work with a gate in the middle. Mrs. Walker, finding no one in the court, opened the trellis gate and looked into the garden, forgetting all other matters in following the bent of her natural genius " for keeping people in order." The wall of the kitchen garden, which separated it from Mary's little garden, was to the right of this back court, and there in the pathway near the wall

stood, within twenty yards of her, as still as
a statue, a tall human figure of supernatural
height, with the light from Mary's passage
window streaming full on the upper part of
it. " She saw it as plain as a pikestaff. The
head was uncovered, and the face looked
ghastly white and mournful, and it had its
arms straight down by its sides like a figure
taken out of a coffin, and clinging to one of
its hands was a large black object that
might be a vampire." Mrs. Walker gave a
loud shriek, and rushed panting into the
house; then, bursting into the kitchen
upon the astonished servants, she fell to the
ground in violent hysterics.

Harrison was immediately sent for, and
prayers had to be stopped—Jenkins going
off to inform Miss Doddingstead that Mrs.
Walker had fallen down in a fit. This
incapable person soon arrived on the scene

herself to take command. It was long before they could bring the housekeeper round, but they at last got her into bed, and the unfortunate Ruth had to stay with her all night with the door locked. In the morning she refused to get up, and, sending for Miss Doddingstead, announced her immediate departure.

Harrison on this went up also to see her. He had heard that Lady Gentlebird was again changing her housekeeper, and he suggested that Mrs. Walker should write a "proper letter" to her ladyship, and offer herself to be taken back again; in the mean time he would send her over to his sister at Deal, where she might take some warm sea baths that "would restore the quality of her blood," which she was so convinced had been altered.

This arrangement being agreed to, Har-

rison forwarded Mrs. Walker's letter—
which he took care to see was "proper"—
nine miles across country by Mr. Spillett
himself, for diplomatic reasons, mounted on
the sturdy Rusty Jack, to Lady Gentlebird's
peaceful mansion.    Now that his enemy
was beaten and in full retreat he could be
generous; though he had no objection to
"returning her ladyship's bad coin on her
ladyship's hands if her ladyship was silly
enough to take it back again."

# CHAPTER II.

MARY, this same morning, was in her room in deep consultation with Spillett. She had heard the loud shriek in the garden the night before, and had been in an agony of mind lest her lover should be discovered, for she did not doubt it was he. One of her windows, as we are aware, looked into the little garden from the corner of the room that formed a recess, and of late she had been in the habit of sitting here in the evening gazing at the sky, not closing the shutters until just before going to bed. On the

day before, however, she had the shutters
closed at dark, still sitting near it late in
the evening with a book in her hand.
The window in the little hall outside had
neither shutter nor curtain, but only iron
bars, and Mary had also wished to ex-
tinguish the lamp that burnt near it; but
Spillett having declared she should break
her neck on the stairs, it had remained
lighted as usual, and it is to be feared the
unhappy ghost of the garden had been
gazing at this window, thinking it was his
mistress's actual bower.

Mary was in great agitation of mind,
balancing between many feelings. She
wanted to convey to her lover that he
must leave the place at once—above all
things, that he was not to come about the
house like a ghost in the night. She
could not make up her mind to write to

him; she was gratified at his constant devotion, and yet he must be sent away.

"If you could only have seen him, Spillett!" she said in desperation.

Spillett did not quite like the idea of "prowling about like a ghost" herself, even on such a romantic errand; but her inventive genius was not long at fault.

"I can walk over to the Spike Farm after lunch, Miss Mary, about the Colonel's cheeses if you like; Mr. Harrison wants to send somebody who can blow them up a little, and very likely I may meet him somewhere, as he is about there all day they say. But I would send him a little note, ma'am. Poor fellow! he's really worth something, or he wouldn't take so much trouble. Most gentlemen like him would sit down and smoke over it, with brandy and soda water. *I* think it's very cruel that you don't see him just once, now he is down here; he will get into a slow depression, and think you don't really care about him, and fall ill or something."

"It's quite *impossible*, Spillett!" said Mary, with her face on fire. "I should never forgive myself!"

"It's wonderful how people who are brought up as ladies and gentlemen work their love affairs," said Spillett. "Of course, I know one mustn't jump into a man's mouth, and that we must be as nice and as difficult to catch as you kittens; but we mustn't get into a fog of fastidious fancyings till it's worse than hide-and-seek on a common. When you are quite sure a man wants to marry you, and you are quite sure you want to marry him, and he is good and nice and all that, and you say no to him when you are told to do so by those in authority over you, because they don't fancy him themselves, it's very like starving yourself to death to keep company with your elders that have got no appetite; and even St. Paul himself, when he tells children to obey their parents, gives them a loophole to save their consciences by, and he ties people up pretty tight too—particularly woman—which always makes me think he must have been crossed in his love affairs; but if you come to that, there is always somebody who wants to prevent your doing everything— except going to church! And, of course, Miss Mary, I know we must listen to our elders, because they can see over the tops of our heads, but not when they look asquint from born obstinacy like——But I don't think Captain Wyldeman will ever go away till he's seen you; he is not the sort of man to be frightened by the Colonel or any one, or he wouldn't have come about here at night, and you'll have to see him sooner or later."

"Spillett!" murmured poor Mary, writhing under this sharp goading to go a way she did not approve of, blaming her hero in her heart one moment and pardoning him the next as she thought of his boldness and constancy, and yet thinking that her grandfather would be more prejudiced against him than ever if he discovered this rash step, "I must write to Captain Huntingcroft," she said, "and entreat him to stop his coming to the garden whatever he does; but now he knows that he has been seen, I should hope he would keep away for my sake."

"You must not be too sure of that, Miss Mary. Men, when they are very much in love, are like flies after sugar—nothing keeps them away."

"Then, you must try and find him, Spillett, and entreat him for my sake not to come near the house again. I know he thought he would never be seen at that time of night or he would not have come, poor fellow, as he is most considerate, and obeys me about everything, and never wrote again when I told him not to; and it is Captain Huntingcroft, I am sure, who has encouraged him to come down here—he declared he would have carried me off himself with a coach and six horses," she said, smiling through her trouble.

"And that is what I should have done too, Miss Mary," said Spillett, with a high colour suddenly mounting to her face; "only I should have taken you off across country on the back of a horse behind me, like that picture of the lady and gentleman in the Colonel's room."

"Ridiculous, Spillett! We should have been caught by the telegraph directly, and laughed at for the rest of our lives!"

"That's just it, Miss Mary; as father says, we live in a mean, spy-paper age, and there is nothing big or romantic left about anybody. People have all got so frightened of each other and things being known, they daren't do a thing that others don't do; he says that comes of too long a peace. We want a good big fight to make people men and women again."

"I don't think so, Spillett," said Mary with some warmth. "I am sure grandpapa does what he likes, without thinking of any one's opinion."

"Oh yes, ma'am, I am sure *he* does, and no fear! But, as father always says, the

Colonel is one of the real good old gentle-men sort—in that way—who have all got the same ways and manners at the top, but do just as they like at the bottom ; but the new sorts now, they are all jumps and bobs, and for making believe to be inde-pendent outside, and are just like a parcel of sheep at the bottom when it really comes to doing anything. If the Prince of Wales was a bachelor now, and was to carry off some young lady on the back of a horse behind him into the moon, do you think, ma'am, there wouldn't be a hundred others to go and do the same thing directly ? And no one then would say they were ridiculous, I am sure ! "

" No, no, Spillett ; people are only learn-ing at last to follow those who see best. This is an age of young Education leading old Ignorance like a blind man."

"Oh yes, I know, Miss Mary; but that's what you read in your books. I don't believe in books, though I read a good many too. I believe more in seeing and hearing. But father reads a good deal as well, and he says it's nothing but an age of hurrying and chivying about, and it's a regular game at knocking over old things, and laughing at them, and seeing who can knock down the most."

"You are wrong, Spillett! The world is full of old abuses and shams that are better · away; and new ideas and things also are interesting, and give one something fresh to think about and see," said Mary rather hotly, the Doddingstead combativeness at last aroused.

"Whoop!" cried Solomon.

"That I don't deny, ma'am. No one likes anything fresh and new better than I do

—particularly in dress; but what I do
say, Miss Mary, is, that people who run hot
after every new fangle and things that will
be forgotten in a year, don't know the real
value of things that have stood up strong
for any time, in spite of the see-sawing
there always is in most people's minds
about nearly everything. But it's most of
it vanity and to splash up a bit to astonish
you and that you may look at them—though
it's only your second-rates who do that
after all; for Madame de Gros is very sharp
in seeing what people are, and I've heard
her say she always knew really first-rate
people in any line by their liking to be
quiet more than by any other thing else,
and not wanting to change things unless
they were really bad. They paid much the
most regularly, too, and that's why she was
so sharp in finding them out for another

thing. Mr. Harrison says also, Miss Mary, those who turn up their noses at everything that is old haven't got what he calls 'the bump of attachment,' and will desert you to-morrow for a new face; and if they are envious, it's just those people who will be wanting soon to drag the queen off her throne, and be sticking up Mr. Smith and his wife in her place—till they want to change them too,—and be making the bishops and archbishops preach in a chapel like the dissenting ministers, and having poor people's children taught astronomy and navigation, and logic and all that, without their knowing there is such a thing as the Bible in particular, or turning the heel of a stocking and such like, as it ought to be, which is wanted as much, I say, in a poor man's house as meat and firing. And what's the good of stuffing galloping notions into poor people's heads that must always be poor—do what you will—and go afoot ? It's like giving a man a saddle who hasn't got a horse; it only makes him a conceited halfway sort of thing, and discontented into the bargain, when he thinks he ought to ride, and he never will do anything but walk ; it's like—— "

" Spillett ! " burst in Mary, " you are most illiberal ! You would have burnt people at the stake, if you had lived in old days. Why shouldn't poor people have as good an education as the rich, and rise to be lord chancellors and prime ministers, if they like ? And as for what you say about the queen, I don't see much harm in that either, when the country is flooded with poverty and heavy taxes—the thousands and thousands that might go to the good of the people, if the taxes were lightened, that are now wasted in setting up idols for fashionable people to curtsey before, whom no one else is allowed to come within a mile of, and which we could do very well without. How can clergymen get up into the pulpit every Sunday and preach about humility and following the example of Christ, and then be busying their brains all the rest of the week—as many of them do in London and the large towns—to get some title or dignity to set them up above their neighbours? I would have no rank or title anywhere except in the army and navy —and you are a bigoted Tory, Spillett!"

At this sounding accusation, Spillett lost her temper.

"Whoop! *Naughty* bird! Water!" cried Solomon.

"I am sure you are a red hot Republican-Radical, Miss Mary; and it would make

the Colonel's hair stand on end to hear
you; and you have learnt all that from
Miss Van Tromp, who had got the regular
cantankerous foreign look of wishing to
drag everybody down into the same boat!"

"Jenny, I think you forget yourself!"
said this red hot Republican-Radical and
apostle of humility, with a fine flash of
aristocratic pride in her eyes, which
changed however to sadness as the name
of her old governess recalled her former
happiness and her present trouble.

Spillett was going to retort, but Mary's
expression brought her back to the real
business in hand, and with an affectionate
look of protection, she said, "I am very
sorry, I am sure, Miss Mary, to be setting
up my opinion against yours; but you
wouldn't have me say what I don't think,
and be smothering you up with pomatum,

as Mrs. Jenkins does Miss Doddingstead.
But we have something else to do besides
fighting over what is men's business, after
all, that we can never touch; and I'll find
Captain Wyldeman, and stop his coming
here, if he's to be found, and if he is to be
stopped, which is quite another matter; for
young men in love, if the door is shut in
their faces, are as bold and sly as burglars
—that is, if they are of the right sort—and I
should never be surprised to find him sitting
down here quietly in your room, Miss Mary,
and teasing Solomon till you came in!"

Mary looked alarmed at this Don Juan-
like idea, which so suddenly ended this
most unexpected political storm.

"But you must give me a note to him,
Miss Mary, if it is only three lines, for I
am sure he won't listen to me else; and he
will wonder, perhaps, what business I have

to be meddling, and that it is the Colonel who is at the bottom of it after all."

At length Mary consented to write the following :—

"I entreat you not to come near the house again, and to leave immediately.

"M."

As soon as Spillett had finished her early dinner, she dressed herself with care, and departed for the Spike Farm.

After she had gone, Mary sat down for a short time and cried bitterly ; then, starting up, she tried to occupy herself with her usual pursuits. She opened her box of colours to set her palette, but finding herself squeezing out the same colours several times over in the wrong places, she threw it down in disgust, and going to her piano, she tried one of Handel's songs. She

had a clear sweet voice, and sang Handel
with earnest simplicity and a feeling for
its sublime stateliness and rhythm most
unusual in any young person who is not
a trained professional in these days. Her
singing charmed the few connoisseurs who
heard her, and kept the servants in delight
at her door, when Spillett would allow them
to remain there. (Spillett herself did not
admire Handel. This conservative young
person oddly enough declared he reminded
her of old bores and things dead and
buried.) But no—what a converting fire
is love!—she could not get on with that
either; and for the first time in her life
felt almost as unsympathetic towards her
grand old favourite as Spillett. Closing
her piano with an impatient bang, that
set Solomon listening with all his might
to study this new sound, she took up

some needlework; but even that excellent
tranquillizer of feminine vibrations failed,
and she decided to go down into the
little garden and look after her pets, which
she had neglected the whole day. When
she got to the bottom of the stairs, a tall
figure, who strangely resembled the ghost
of the garden, came out of the little summer
house, and stood before her.

" Mary ! "

" Frank ! Captain Wyldeman ! How
could you—how dare you come in here ? "

" Mary, I should have died if I had
not seen you ! Don't be unkind to me ! "

" How *very* imprudent—how *wrong* of
you ! If my grandfather only knew ! "

" Mary, I entreat you to speak to me
for only a few minutes. If you knew how I
love you, and how wretched I am at not
seeing you or hearing anything from you

for so long ! I think of nothing but you night and day ! " As he spoke, he advanced towards her.

But Mary flew up the stairs and spoke to him over the rail.

" Captain Wyldeman, if you really care for me, you would not put me to such pain by coming here. I wonder that you have not more consideration for me, if you have none for yourself. You must indeed leave the garden directly, and never come here again."

" Oh, Mary ! don't go away like that ; we may never see each other again ! I have got leave of absence, and I am going abroad almost directly ; and I am even thinking of leaving the regiment—my life is so miserable now."

Mary remained a moment silent, shaken by this news.

"Dear Mary, I entreat you!" he said again, with such manly love in his voice and in his fine blue eyes as he looked up to her, that there is no saying what request she might have granted if he had not rashly advanced towards the stairs ; whereupon young madam, who would and who would not, shot within her door and drew the bolts, as much upon herself as against her lover.

# CHAPTER III.

## THE HERO TRAMPLES LITTLE ANIMALS TO DEATH, THE GHOST OF MR. GREGO APPEARS TO THE KING OF ZANZIBAR, AND MARY FIGHTS ANOTHER BATTLE.

"The Little Sack, Wednesday Evening.

"DEAR H. D.,

"I have seen her and spoken to her! But what an interview—it lasted about three seconds! I will tell you exactly how it all happened. And I hope to be more lively and cheerful this time, though you are a little wrong to say I write nothing but 'doleful dumps.' But it is awfully good of you, all the same, to read my long letters; but you don't

know how much I feel about it all." (It was
certainly not for want of hearing about it!
But our hero was in the usual fog of
amiable delusions generated by ardent love.)

" I went again to the garden last night,
and was looking up at her windows, when
a huge female came out of some back-yard
place close to me, and, letting off a scream
that would bring the devil from his Sunday
dinner, she bolted in again. I could not
think what she took me for; but I find now,
as you shall hear, she thought I was one of
the twenty ghosts Mrs. Crippin says they
have at the Manor. Some fellows then
came running from the stables—which it
appears in this strange old place are somewhere in the kitchen-garden,—so I had to
spring over the nearest wall, and landed
on something which must have been a
cage full of little animals, as there was a

great squeaking, and a lot of small brutes
bolted that I could have sworn were rats by
the smell of them, if it were possible ! The
place was partly lighted by a window with
a candle burning in it, and I thought it
best for a time to hide in a sort of low shed
there was in the corner. It had straw in
it, so I crept in and sat down, and was
thinking about Mary so near to me and
yet not able even to see her for an instant,
when I felt something pulling gently at
my hair, and on looking round, I saw a
white figure standing quite close to me.
By old Crocker ! I thought it was one of
the ghosts. I started up as if I had been
sitting on a viper, and my head went
through the roof, and I carried off the
whole building on my back like Samson ;
then I got my foot through another cage
or something, and I am sure I trod some

little animal to death. At last I got free of the shed on my back, but I lost my hat, and couldn't find it anywhere again! I then discovered a door in a wall at the bottom of the garden, which was only bolted inside. I got that open, and nearly broke my neck down a flight of steps into a dark lane. I pulled the door to again, and on walking a little way I made out the old church; and then I knew where I was, and it flashed upon me that it must have been *her* garden and *her* pets that I had been trampling to death! Will she ever forgive me? Just like my luck!

"But I have not half finished my story yet. Well, I got home all safe, except that Mrs. Crippin stared at me for having no hat, and looked as black as thunder again for my keeping her up so late at night—10.30 only —or eleven at the most! But this respectable old dragon, I find, likes to retire to her den at eight o'clock, and I am sure she is at her wits' ends to know what I am doing down here, and why I stay out so late at nights. I heard her telling Mary Tumber this evening she feared I was up to no good, and that she had better keep her door locked!

" I was dreadfully annoyed about Mary's garden, and I went to the door in the lane again this afternoon to see if it was still open or if there was any chance of my finding her there. I found the door just as I left it, and I could not resist the temptation of stealing in. What do you think was the ghost? It was her white goat that you told me about! Don't laugh! I am sure you would have been frightened, too, in such an old ghost-warren of a place. Well! there was the goat tied up on the

straw, and his house lying a wreck just
as I left it. My hat was underneath it.
Evidently no one had been there. The
goat began to make such a baaing when it
saw me, that I got into a summer-house, as
I was afraid they would spot me from the
windows, though, to say the truth, I should
not have much minded, except for her
sake, as I should uncommonly like to fight
that old turkey-cock of a Colonel and all
his household ; it would have done me
good, I am sure. But, *revenons à nos
chevreuils.* I had not been there long when
I heard her light little step on the wooden
stairs. I know it so well! There is not
a woman in the world who treads as lightly
as she does! You should have seen her
face when she saw me! I never saw her
look so handsome; her eyes flashed at me
like a gun going off, and I felt almost

afraid of her. Gentle as she is, she has got something of the thunder and lightning sort about her when she chooses; and she can look so serious! I always wonder how she came to like such a fellow as I am. She blew me up like anything for coming there, and I couldn't put in a word or get near her. If I could only have got my arms round her! But she flew up the stairs like a bird, and before I could get her to hear a word or say she would see me again she was gone, and I heard her bolt the door at the top. With one hat on my head, and another in my hand, I must have looked an awful donkey at that moment!

"But I have not done yet. I find I have got another friend at court, who backs me up, I think, nearly as much as you do, and that is her maid, to whom I used to send her letters, and who she told me something

about. I thought she was some middle-aged
old faithful, all devotion and tiresomes. Not
a bit of it! She is a charming little dare-
devil, and quite young. I must tell you how
I saw her. I was going back by the lane,
ready to shoot myself, when I saw coming
towards me an uncommonly good-looking
young woman most prettily dressed. She
reminded me of a servant in an old play,
but she did not look quite like a servant
either. I could not imagine who she could
be. I was going to pass her, when she
pulled me up short with, 'Captain Wyldeman, I think, sir?' I took off my hat to
her as if she were a duchess, and said,
'Yes, I am Captain Wyldeman.' Whereupon she pulled a note out of her pocket
and said, 'I have got a letter for you, sir,
from my young mistress.' I opened the
note. It was just one cruel line from Mary

to tell me to leave directly. That was all! I suppose I must have looked like a cur with his tail between his legs, for her maidship at once proceeded to give me as nice a little lecture as ever you heard for coming about the place like a ghost on stilts—frightening everybody into hysterics till family prayers had to be stopped—and getting her young mistress into trouble, if the Colonel found it out; and that wasn't the way, unless I meant to carry her off like a man. And that ' you might as well try to get to heaven by staring up at the sky, as to get a young lady by gazing up at her closed windows.' At last she became a little more civil, and said she was quite on my side, though she was nobody, and that if I stuck to Mary, the Colonel would give in yet—he was much too fond of her to say no for ever —and that I was not to think of going

away because I was told to do so, but that
I was to keep away from the house for the
present, as the servants were on the watch;
and that I had better write to Mary again
under cover to her as before. What do
you think? Mary is such a serious girl at
the bottom, and so delicate in her feelings,
and after the way she wrote to me last
time, I always feel as if I might crush or
break something that could never be set
right again, and yet that is why I am so
fond of her. I am sure, from what I have
seen of them, serious women are the best,
and the most loving and true when they
once belong to you; I have noticed that
several times. You remember Di Wilson,
that the fellows were so afraid of, and how
happy she has made Campbell? He swear
by her now, though it took him so long to
pluck up courage enough to propose.

Altogether that stunning maid has cheered me tremendously. I wondered if I ought to give her a good tip; but I believe she would have thrown it in my face, so I shook hands with her, which seemed to please her. She is no common girl that, and will make a splendid little wife to some fellow some day, as I am sure she is good too. I told her how it was I was forced to get into Mary's garden, and she promised to explain; but she said 'it didn't much matter—most women liked being trampled on one way or another—except in their dress?'

"I wish you could run down for a bit. It's awfully dull, particularly at night. There is not a book in the house except one called 'Crab Robinson'—a new cookery book, I think, but I have not looked into it—and a big old Bible with pictures in it.

I have taken to reading that, and you can't think how interesting it is. I don't think I ever read the Bible seriously before. My dear mother was too anxious about me, and I had religion and all that so pumped into me when I was young, that I got disgusted with it; and that, I believe, is the great reason why some fellows almost hate the sight of the Bible. That fellow St. Paul was a splendid fellow!—only read the Acts of the Apostles! How I should like to have heard him preach; and what a general he would have made; and he was such an awfully kind fellow, too! And then Ruth! Jacob was rather an ass" (did our hero mean Rachel?); " but it is very interesting to read about him and how he was done in his love affairs. I am sure Mary is religious, and she would think me a dreadful heathen if she knew all, but I must coach up a little. Besides, I begin to like it now. I don't think I should make a bad parson, after all, if I was properly crammed for it. Mary is too good for me, I feel that, and I mean to try and be more worthy of her. Don't shout! Wait till you are in love, old fellow, with a real, good, sincere-minded girl that's not all kites and ready-made sweets to every fellow, but one who you are sure means what she says and is not acting being nice —which only makes a fellow feel small when he sees it's the same to everybody. Ah! how good I will be to Mary if she ever belongs to me! I will guard her like some tender and beautiful morning flower that would close at a breath of cold wind! Don't say, now, I have written you a doleful letter. It is only thinking of Mary that makes me so sad. There is not another

girl like her in the whole world; and I
fear my luck is not good enough ever to
get her! What do you advise now? It is
all very well for you to say, ' See her!' but
I can't get near her; if I do, she won't stay.
I feel very small, dodging about here like
an escaped convict. I can't say I much like
it—but, as you say, all is fair in love and
war.

" Ever yours,

" F. W.

" P.S.– That reminds me of one thing I
have forgotten to mention. As I was creep-
ing round the outside wall the other night,
I distinctly heard some one fire off a gun
or a pistol out of one of the windows of
the house. That must be the ghost of the
murderer Mrs. Crippin told me about. He
shot his own son out of the window, and
still goes on firing out of the window at

night, she says, when anything is going to happen. How can Mary live in such a dreadful old place! I wonder what is going to happen?"

Spillett, after the events related, found her young mistress in great agitation and excitement, and her habitual gentleness and tranquillity were turned to restless and conflicting emotion. She was angry, she was pleased, she was alarmed and yet hopeful at such constancy and love ; and she was sad at the thought of her lover's departure for the Continent.

"But it is no use your being angry with him, ma'am. The idea of a man being afraid of anything or stopping at anything if he really cares for you! I think it is very nice of him, giving up his pipe and his armchair, and coming out and standing

in the cold just for the chance of getting
a sight of you, and worshipping an old
stone wall because you are on the other
side of it—and only think of his jumping
over your wall like that! I like a man to
be big and strong. I shouldn't much mind
being carried off by a giant into his castle,
if he wasn't ugly and didn't mean to eat
one. I would rather have that than a
poor polished-to-death creature, who thinks
of nothing but being 'correct,' and what
other people will say about him—and
afraid of you into the bargain!"

"I shall tell my grandfather, Spillett. I
will not deceive him again for anything,"
said Mary seriously.

"Don't think of such a thing, ma'am!
Do you want to have all the men fighting
each other—or, what's worse, appearing
before the magistrates, and the whole

affair in the papers? The Colonel would never consent then, you may be quite sure; there wouldn't be a chance for you! You didn't invite him to come; and I don't see that you have done anything to confess. If you want to be courageous, you had much better stick up to the Colonel again, and make him consent. He will, if you go on long enough. There isn't a man living can beat a woman if she will only stick to her point. Men are stronger than we are in many ways, but they can't stick on to a thing as we do. You see a man can knock another man on the head if he holds on too fast, but they daren't do that with us; and that's our little privilege that a woman should never lose sight of, and I am sure a man gets tired of saying no much sooner than a woman does."

Mary had all the keen dread of a public

scandal, which belongs to a sensitive high-
bred race, and Spillett's arguments pre-
vailed ; she even decided to make another
attempt to gain her grandfather's consent.

" And the queen, Miss Mary ? We must
go down and see what *your* giant has been
trampling on ; but he is a fine-built young
gentleman, I must say, if he doesn't get
too stout some day. I should like to have
seen him, though, floundering about there
in the dark in your garden ! "

The two young women lighted a lantern
and went down into the garden. Mary's
first care was to see that the door was
again bolted, and she got a hammer and
drove in two nails for further security.
Great was her astonishment when she saw
the wrecked state of the house she had
built for her goat. The rats in the cage
had disappeared altogether, but old Poacher

seemed to have escaped death, though his
cage was crushed in over his head, as if
a giant indeed had been trampling about
there.    Spillett laughed with her clear
voice, and said, " men were very like cattle
when they hadn't got a woman to prick
them up and to remind them of what they
were about."

During their absence a little event of
importance to our heroine occurred upstairs.
The ghost of Mr. Grego appeared to the
King of Zanzibar.

The monkey had been struggling on.
With Harrison's skilful assistance and his
own native vigour he had been making
a resolute fight with death ; and if he
could only have been transported suddenly
to his native island for a little visit of ten
days or a fortnight, he would have probably
recovered all but his lost eye.    He had,

however, been still confined to Mary's bedroom. Between this room and the sitting-
room were double doors, seldom used in
the winter—Mary passing out into the
little hall and entering her bedroom by
another door. In the agitation and excitement of the events just recorded, Mary had
left her bedroom door open, and Spillett
the door of the sitting-room. The king,
comfortably installed in his house, quickly
spied the open door. Such a tempting
prospect of adventure was not to be resisted,
and he soon managed to undo the door of
his house and spring to the ground. He
first jumped into Mary's bed, and pulling
out her pillow threw it off on to the floor ;
he then crept under the bedclothes, but
finding the sheets too cold, he came out
again and sprang from the bed to the toilet-
table ; after he had upset everything there,

and tasted a pot of cold cream, some of which he rubbed on his face, he jumped down again and made for the door. It was not long before he found his way into the sitting-room, attracted by the light of the fire.

After the windows were closed in the evening, Solomon always relapsed into silent contemplation—whether of a self-educational or retrospective nature no one could say; it could only be observed that he was very still and solemn, and did not go to sleep.

The king gambolled into the room, his tail in the air, delighted with his freedom and change, and such a prospect of mischief all to himself; but Solomon's fine ear soon detected an unusual sound. "Naughty bird!" he exclaimed, with an exact imitation of Spillett, much after the manner of Mr. Grego.

The king sat for a few seconds in the middle of the room, with his hands in the air transfixed with terror and astonishment. There was the same cage in the same place, and the same bird with the same voice. He gave a sharp shriek like the rasping of hard iron, and, flying out of the door, he returned to Mary's room and hid himself under the bed.

Mary, when she entered her room to dress for dinner, at once perceived who had been at work there. The monkey's house was empty, but where could he be? After a search, he was discovered under the bed in the far corner, crouching against the wall and trembling violently. She and Spillett got him out, and placed him again in his house, but he only shrieked piteously, and tried to hide himself under the straw. Mary was certain he was very

ill again ; and the unfortunate Harrison
was summoned in haste as he was attend-
ing to his preparations for dinner. He
thought that the monkey had only caught
a fresh chill by going out into the passages,
and treated him accordingly ; being too
much in haste to consider the matter very
closely.

The Colonel that night at dinner was
unusually cheerful. The clock went well—
remarkably well ; he had been giving a
final touch to it that morning, but he did
not descant with his usual fulness of detail
on the exact nature of the engineering
difficulties he had encountered and over-
come, although his granddaughter forced
herself to give her accustomed attention
to his narrative, having a genius that way
nerself. Then, Lady Grandison having
accepted the Coppice Wood, he had had

the delightful occupation of riding over
there to see about the necessary repairs,
and Mary learnt for the first time the
remarkably contumacious character of a
lead roof, that was no sooner repaired in
one place than it persisted in leaking in
another, and how truly wonderful were the
insatiable demands of an old house for
repairs when once you began.   Even the
very coal-cellar wanted a new brick floor
and two coats of whitewash.   But he had
given orders to spare no expense, and the
place was to be made as cheerful as if it
were " for a young married couple."   The
drawing-room was to be white and gold—
Tumber declared it must be that, " if it was
to look bridal."  Miss Doddingstead thought
it would have been better if it had remained
oak as it was before—the Colonel thought
the same ; but that fellow Tumber was as

obstinate as a Yorkshireman about it.   He
said oak colour was only fit for gentlemen who hunted and filled the room
with tobacco smoke, and ladies liked
things to look as different from men's as
possible—something that will go with
their dresses.

"Tumber has got a very pretty wife,
for I have seen her," said the Colonel; "and
I dare say he knows all about it, so I did
not interfere very much.   Men who marry
pretty women learn many things—I have
long observed that."

"Yes, indeed," said his daughter; "they
learn to be kept in order, and that they
are not the only men in the world!"

"Well done, Augusta!" said the
Colonel, looking at her with great astonishment.

Mary bent down over her plate to hide a

smile.    She knew where this third-hand
wisdom came from.

" I hear from Harrison Lady Gentlebird
has settled to take Mrs. Walker back again.
But why did she part with her ? " he said,
when the servants had left the room.

" It was the other servants, Jenkins
thinks," said Miss Doddingstead.    " She
will be a great loss to us ; you can't think
how clean she has made everything, and
how well she has kept Harrison and
Spillett in their places."

" Umph ! " said the Colonel.    " You had
better let Harrison find some one for himself this time—he is a clever fellow, and is
a much better judge of the matter than we
are."

" I know who Harrison wants to make
housekeeper," said his daughter, " and that
is Jenny Spillett.    But she is much too

young—it is absurd! And Jenkins says she
would not stay to be under her. I think
Jenkins would make a good housekeeper;
she says she can take care of me just the
same."

" Ridiculous!" said the Colonel. " She
has no more brains than a stuffed goose,
and if she does not like it, let her go. I
don't see why Jenny Spillett should not do
very well. I rather like the idea; it will
please her father immensely,—and the
Spilletts are not common people, you must
remember. If she does not quarrel with
Harrison, she will hold her own well
enough, young as she is."

" But Spillett's father is always interfering, and Jenkins says he is much too
thick with Mr. Croucher to be quite
honest," said Miss Doddingstead.

" There never was such a good honest

fellow as Spillett, and I don't believe a word of it," said the Colonel hotly; "and his daughter is like him, though she has got a tongue of her own—but that cuts both ways when you come to keeping others in order. What do you say, Mary? Could she look after you as well?"

"Oh yes, grandpapa; I need very little waiting on. I should be very pleased indeed!"

Miss Doddingstead still offered a feeble opposition, which only made the Colonel more determined to promote Spillett.

"I will talk to Harrison about it," he said; and the ladies retired.

Miss Doddingstead went off to the drawing-room for her accustomed nap, and Mary waited in the hall with a beating heart until she thought the great pipe had been lighted and its soothing effects allowed to operate. She then opened the door gently, a little to the surprise of the Colonel, which was increased still more when she knelt down on the ground near him and put her hands on his knees. He first wondered if the monkey had got lost again, or if it was something about Spillett, but her face looked so grave and earnest, he began to fear it was " that fellow " again.

"Dear grandpapa, you won't be angry with me!" she said, looking up into his face beseechingly, "but there is something I must tell you."

" Well, my dear," he said very gravely.

"Captain Wyldeman is staying at the Little Sack, and he is going abroad for a long time, and he entreats me to see him once more before he goes, to say good-bye."

The Colonel had so much confidence in

Mary's truth and prudence, that he did not press her to know how she obtained this information.

" What business has he to be coming down here, after you have intimated my wishes to him ?  It is most indelicate and forward, and I am surprised that Hunting-croft should encourage him, after what passed between us on the subject !"  He looked down at her with a darkening face.

" But, grandpapa, he says he shall go out of his mind if you do not give your consent !"

" What does that matter to me ?  He should have thought of that before."

" But he could not help being fond of me directly he saw me, he says ; and we ought never to have been allowed to see each other if it was so wrong his liking me."  Tears began to come in her eyes.

The Colonel again swore inwardly at

his own indiscretion. "My dear, my dear," he said kindly, putting his hand on her head, "it cannot be, indeed, it cannot be!"

"But, grandpapa, I shall never, never be happy again, for I *do* care for him so!"

Old Shot now came and joined the group, putting his head on the Colonel's knee and also looking up at him with pleading eyes, which, however, had a tinge of jealousy in them rather than advocacy.

"My dear child, that is all nonsense! If he had not come down here and planted himself near you, you would have got over it—as you will now, when he is gone."

"No, no, grandpapa!—never, never! I have tried very hard to forget him"— her tears and sobs came thick—"but—but it is always the same. I can *never* care for any one else now!"

"Stuff and nonsense, Mary!" said the Colonel, starting up from his chair and knocking the big pipe to the ground, more angry with himself than with her, and cut to the heart by her earnest distress. "You talk like a schoolgirl! Why you are barely eighteen!"

"Oh! don't be hard on me, dear grand-papa!" she said, trying to get hold again of his knees.

"It cannot be! it cannot be!" he exclaimed, endeavouring to break away from her.

"If poor papa had only been alive!" said Mary in her desperation, still clinging to him.

This stung the Colonel very deeply. He had often reflected if her parents had been alive, would this have happened, and how would they have acted under the circumstances? He would have given his right hand at that moment to have been able to conquer his repugnance to the match, and a feather would have turned the scale.

Mary divined the trembling of the balance; but alas, for inexperience and candour in a great political crisis! she made a fatal mistake. "I am sure you would like him—they say he is not the least like Sir John, and that *he* is not so bad as you think!"

This brought back all the Colonel's recollections of the man whom he knew well to be little better than a scoundrel, and was irritating also as throwing a doubt on his judgment and justice; the meddling of others, also, in a matter on which he allowed no one to interfere, roused his combativeness.

"I tell you, Mary, it is quite impossible,

quite impossible!" he said, beating the air
with his hands, and dragging her on her
knees across the room to the door as she
clung to him! "I forbid you to have any
further communication with him!"

Breaking from her, he got out into the
hall, and went straight to his own room
and locked the door. Mary retreated
slowly upstairs, with her face between her
hands, and with bitter sobs declared "she
would never ask him anything again!"

Half an hour afterwards the Colonel
stole out and fetched his pipe, and remained
smoking in his room until an advanced
hour of the night. Neither he nor Mary
appeared at prayers, and Harrison was
much perplexed to know what could have
happened.

"Had he and Miss Mary been having
a serious to do at last over the clock and

the monkey? She was a regular Dodding-stead, gentle as she was; and, as Jenny Spillett says, 'what can you expect from game fowl but fighting?'"

# CHAPTER IV.

## CRACKSKULL COMMON AND THE FOUR-CROSS WAY.

MARY had a restless and tearful night, which ended in a deep sleep, in which she dreamt that she was in the midst of a great crowd. At a short distance her grandfather and Captain Wyldeman were talking to each other, but the crowd was so thick she could not get through it to speak to them. In an agony, she tried to call out, but could not utter a sound—when she awoke, and found Spillett opening the shutters of her window. Her sweet face looked very mournful as it lay on the pillow, bedded in the masses of her glowing hair, which curled like serpents around her, and her rich dark eyes, in the half-light of the dimity curtained bed, had that deep sadness which appeals to the strong and good with the subtle charm that lies about misfortune. Spillett had a fine expression as she glanced at her young mistress.

Mary did not seem disposed to enter into conversation. She and Spillett had exhausted the night before all that was to be said for the moment on the present situation. There seemed nothing but a dead wall of despair before her, with little hope of ever passing it. "She would never see him or hear his cheerful voice again." At length she said gently—

"I think I'll have some tea, Spillett. I

shall not get up just yet. I don't want anything to eat; but before you go, just look at the king and see how he is."

Before going to bed on the previous night she had peeped into his house, and he seemed quietly asleep, curled up in a corner with his head buried between his hands.

"Oh, Miss Mary!" exclaimed Spillett, as she opened the door of the monkey's house and put in her hand, "he is quite cold— and I think he's dead!"

Mary sprang out of bed, her pink feet flying over the carpet. Alas! there could be no doubt about it, her little friend, who of late had been of more value than ever to her, had gone to join the spirits of his happy isle. With all his faults and his one great crime, he had been a most amusing little fellow, ever quaint and original, with a droll perversity that was a constant element of cheerfulness and fun in the somewhat dull old Manor, and he had been associated with some of the happiest years of her girlhood; for is it not those persons and animals who have the most character to whom we attach ourselves the most warmly, even though they have great faults, ay, or it may be worse?

Mary took him out in her arms, and Harrison was summoned from his breakfast, Spillett carrying the king out for him to see. He said there was nothing to be done, and he thought he had been dead for many hours. The king was placed again in his house, and a new handkerchief was spread tenderly over him. Mary then got into bed again, drew the clothes over her head, and sobbed like a child at this accumulation of misfortune.

When Spillett brought up the tea, she was greatly moved with compassion, and she resolved in her heart, "that if she died for it, Miss Mary should marry Captain Wyldeman yet!"

"Never mind, Miss Mary," she said; "Captain Wyldeman isn't dead! and I think he looks pretty tough. I don't think that even love will kill him—though, for the matter of that, I don't believe that there was ever a man or woman either who died really of love yet, though it's nice and romantic for people who write love stories to try to make us think so. Things are not worse than they were; in fact, better, I think. You may be sure you have driven it in more home to the Colonel. He isn't a man, if it's only for the sake of peace and comfort, if he doesn't turn round some fine morning and say, 'Oh, take your man and go to the devil, and do what you like with him '—you'll see ! "

Mary shook her head sadly, with a faint smile ; but she felt a little cheered, though somewhat shocked, by Spillett's confident irreverence.

" Come, Miss Mary ! that's not the way to take trouble, lying in bed like a sick hen over eggs that won't hatch. You had much better get up and come down in the garden with me and bury the king. It's no use keeping him up here and moping over him. It is not like a child—it's only a monkey, after all. Mr. Harrison says he ought to be buried in a four-cross way, as he committed suicide, or hung in chains on Crackskull Common, for a murderer and robber. Where's Crackskull Common, Miss Mary ? I never heard of it near here."

"What *do* you mean, Spillett?" said Mary, rousing herself, and taking the cup of tea out of her hand.

"I mean," said Spillett deliberately, trying to provoke Mary's combativeness, "he must be buried in the middle of the garden, where the four paths meet, and he must have no coffin, and he must have a sharp stake driven through him, because he first committed murder and then he poisoned himself."

"That I certainly won't have, Spillett! He must be buried by the side of Mr. Grego." And she proceeded to eat a slice of bread and butter which Spillett had brought up contrary to orders.

"That won't do, Miss Mary. It will bring poor Mr. Grego out of his grave! No, he belongs to the bad spirits amongst monkeys that answers to our devil, and it would be quite wicked of us to try and stop his going where all bad monkeys ought to go to. Do you think creatures like that, who are nearly as intelligent as we are, haven't a future? I believe that all animals have got something that answers to our soul. When they die there is something goes out of them all of a sudden, that is quite different from their bodies, that's evident—where does that go to? I see no more reason to suppose that dies, than what goes out of us. Besides, they have got power to know when they are doing right and when they are doing wrong; why isn't that intended to prepare them for another world just like ourselves? Who knows? You may be riding your mare in heaven yet, some day; only instead of four legs she'll have a lot of wings!"

"Don't talk nonsense, Spillett," said

Mary quietly, her combativeness too crushed for the present to be easily roused, though she could not help being amused at Spillett's theories. "Even supposing what you say is true, how can anything we do to the body touch the spirit that has flown away?"

"I am not so sure of that, Miss Mary. Spirits are governed by laws, I expect, much more like what they have been accustomed to in real life than we suppose; and before they admit a new spirit, they look back to see how he stood at his death for one thing, just as we should at the certificate of a man's character who has been discharged. I have often thought, when I read the papers, that coroners cheat in a way they will have to answer finely for some day."

"I think I will get up now, Spillett,"

said Mary, feeling decidedly more cheerful after her tea. The theological philosopher then proceeded to prepare her mistress's bath.

"I shall not let you have it quite cold this morning, Miss Mary; I don't believe in cold water in winter. It's only those who have got a skin like a Newcastle navvy's that can warm up again properly, and those who feel things very much have not got that. I don't think Satan himself could stand a cold bath down here in Kent on a winter morning—he's too clever; it's only stupid people who have got their brains in their stomach can do that."

"Spillett, you are out of your mind this morning!"

Spillett laughed and departed to finish her breakfast, which was still waiting for her downstairs, for running away from which she was secretly despised by Jenkins, who thought she didn't know what was due to herself and the rules of service—an important article of which, being literally translated, was as follows, " The sacred hour of meal-time shall not be encroached upon; should your master or mistress, for instance, be so inconsiderate as to take to dying at that inconvenient hour, it is better they should be left to grow cold than your tea and toast." Jenkins however had forgotten her own abject submission at the time of Miss Doddingstead's bad colds and consequent exacting temper.

When Spillett returned from her breakfast, she said, " Mr. Harrison says he shall send his nephew Tom over to Antwerp to get you another monkey, Miss Mary ; he has got the man's address, as he was over at Deal again last summer."

"It's very kind of him," said Mary ; "but I shall never care for another."

" That's nonsense, ma'am ! Monkeys are like men—one is much the same as another, when you are obliged to have them about you ; it all depends upon what you can make of them—and that's interesting, and sharpens up one's wits."

Mary smiled, but thought that Jenny's tongue was running away with her ; and she then proceeded to find something that would do as a coffin for the king.

Spillett having succeeded in her object of " stirring Miss Mary up a bit out of her dumps," did not persist any further in her notions of justice in the matter of coroners' law. "The monkey was just as much of an unsound mind as the rest of them."

A very pretty cedar box lined with rose coloured silk, in which a doll had once

come from Amsterdam having been found,
the little king was deposited therein,
carefully covered by one of Mary's lace
pocket-handkerchiefs, with her cipher in the
corner worked by herself; Spillett slipping
in, when Mary's back was turned, one of
the red feathers out of Mr. Grego's tail,
" to keep him quiet in his grave."

The two young women then went down
into the garden, Mary carrying the box
reverently with both hands. After much
discussion, it was decided an entirely new
graveyard should be formed in the opposite
corner to the one in which Mr. Grego was
laid. The king was deposited at a good
depth, and a little mound was formed over
him in the shape of a grave.

"If I was the Pope or the Archbishop
of Canterbury, Miss Mary, I should give
out a funeral service for animals; there is

something wrong that a creature with such cleverness and intelligence as that should be buried like a stone. I am sure there are many dogs, now, that have got more goodness in them than half the Christians going—and without their wickedness, too. Do you think God intended that all that goodness should go for nothing and end here? I don't, Miss Mary."

"I don't think it matters much how we are buried, Spillett; the ancients had one way, you know, and we have another. It's just a matter of custom and love and respect to those who are gone. But you forget, animals don't think anything about that. They don't grieve over another's death as we do."

"But dogs do, Miss Mary, over a master that's dead, just as much as his own relations, and often much more. I have seen that—and I often wonder you don't have a dog."

" I suppose you think, then, my relations won't grieve for me! But these matters are all settled for us, Jenny, by wiser heads than ours."

" I am not so sure of that, Miss Mary; though we are only babes and sucklings, there is good authority for thinking they see the truth more simply and naturally like than those who have got their heads choked up with too much brains like proud flesh."

The interment of the king having been accomplished, Spillett set Mary to work to restore the goat's house, pulling the wreck to pieces much more than was necessary, " to give her plenty of occupation," and they went on sawing and hammering all the morning.

# CHAPTER V.

### THE VISIT TO PARIS.

WHEN Mary met her grandfather at dinner that evening, he was very kind and cheerful, and he astonished his womenkind by talking a great deal about Paris, as he remembered it in his young days, and then about Brighton. Finally, when the servants left the room, he opened his budget of news. He first told Mary she might inform Spillett she was to be the new housekeeper. He had arranged it all with Harrison. Eliza, who was clever, and had been well trained by his wife, was to be head cook, with a seat in the cabinet council of the housekeeper's room; Ruth was to be kitchen-maid, and a new scullery-maid was to be found. Miss Doddingstead was too accustomed to be overruled to make any further resistance—her chief thought in the matter was, " would Jenkins really go?"

Then the Colonel, after a few ahems, came to some really startling news. He had decided to take them at once to either Brighton or Paris. Which did they think the best? He should start in a day or two?

Mary could not utter a word. Miss Doddingstead thought Brighton would be the best, " the shops were so nice to look at."

" So they are in Paris," said the Colonel. " Yes, Paris will be the best, after all; we will decide on Paris. But when can you be ready?"

Miss Doddingstead thought a week at least would be necessary.

"Nonsense!" said the Colonel; "people never take much luggage when they go abroad. You want another pair of boots and a little change, that's all. Let me see, to-day is Thursday; we will start on Monday, then. That's a famous allowance of time for packing, I am sure. What do you say, Mary?"

"When you like, grandpapa," said Mary faintly.

"We will only take one maid," said the Colonel. "You can take that maid of yours, if you like, Augusta—that will be a little sop for her; but I won't be bothered with two maids. They only quarrel, and one has to be sent home. I well remember that happening. I did rather think of taking Harrison," he continued, " he has not had a holiday for a long time ; but I am afraid the house won't get on without him now poor Mrs. Harrison is gone. That is the worst of Spillett being so young. I suppose I shall have to take John."

" I am sure Spillett will manage very well, grandpapa. It will do poor Harrison a great deal of good. Spillett's father might come into the house."

" True, my dear, I never thought of that. Very good ; then we'll take Harrison." And the ladies retired to carry the great news to their respective maids.

The Colonel was dumb with astonishment the following morning, when Mrs. Spillett, the new housekeeper at Whitepatch Manor, marched demurely into prayers at the head of the household. Having little knowledge of theatrical matters, he had never realized the extraordinary transformation that dress and deportment can make in one and the same person. Spillett appeared in a close-fitting black silk dress, which no one at the Manor had ever seen before. She had altered the usual style of dressing her hair; her rebellious locks were smoothed down into correct propriety, and rose up behind in a most imposing and dignified arrangement fastened with a goodly comb, which must have belonged to her grandmother, and she wore a plain gold brooch, which contained a miniature of her great great grandmother—whom no doubt, judging from the miniature, she strongly resembled. A small gold watch and chain completed her dress. But she looked prettier than ever, for the black was very becoming to her brilliant complexion and hair, and her somewhat full figure looked neat and round in its tight-fitting dark dress; in short, the dress suited her; and one saw at a glance her native superiority to the other servants. The Colonel was so fascinated with his own creation that, as he knelt at the table in his accustomed place near the fire, with the servants in a long row before him, he could hardly keep his eyes off Spillett's back as he read out the morning prayer. Jenkins did not appear. She had not yet made up her mind to walk behind " that dressed up doll."

Spillett entered on her business with remarkable aptitude for the business in hand, and as she did not alter her manner to the other servants, the appointment was on the whole accepted, as her father was much liked and respected by every one, and there had been a dread of having " Mrs. Jenkins and her tale-bearing " placed over them. The honour which the Colonel had conferred on her, however, did not alter her determination " to get to wind-ward of the old gentleman in the matter of Miss Mary if she could." In pursuance of a plan she had in her head, she determined to go over to Canterbury in the afternoon of that day, to see Mrs. Sherlock, who had formerly been maid to Mary's mother. She had remained with Mary until the arrival of Miss Van Tromp, when she married her cousin Sherlock, who held a good situation in a Canterbury brewery, and had a nice little house in a walled garden of his own, about a mile from the town on the road to Ickham. Having no children, Mrs. Sherlock generally took in as a lodger one of the curates of the district, but at this moment her pleasant rooms were vacant. When Spillett arrived at the station, she sent a mysterious note by one of the porters, and then proceeded to Canterbury to find Mrs. Sherlock. She, however, returned to the Manor in time for prayers. Jenkins was still absent.

# CHAPTER VI.

## MRS. SPILLETT IS CAUGHT IN HER OWN TRAP.

On the following morning another catastrophe happened to our heroine. But what are heroines for except to suffer many things; everything, in fact, short of being hung by the neck? But such is the desperate state of affairs in the way of finding a novelty, before long a heroine will probably arrive even at that very last misfortune. Perhaps some one more able than the present writer to make extremes meet may take the hint. It might be made into an excellent picture of the

dismal and dreadful school, given the
necessity to paint it. A charming and
beautiful young woman, falsely accused,
pleads guilty to screen her lover, the real
culprit, and is condemned to go through
the ceremony mentioned above—the piti-
able hound, her lover, who won't come
forward to save her, drinking and gossip-
ping in the Royal Tar round the corner—
the heroism of the heroine, who holds out
to the last moment in her silent self-
sacrifice. A damp, raw, foggy, suicidal
November morning at the hour of eight.
A dreadful bell tolls with a dismal heart-
sinking tone that does the highest credit
to the artist who designed it for its position. The black flag ready to be hoisted
may here be brought in with much effect.
Two pages and a half of sad and gloomy
description of the interior of Newgate,

with æsthetic and sparkling allusions to
that great artist and popular hero of the
gibbet, Jack Sheppard, to break up the
monotony of the deep shadows. There is
no one present to witness this crowning
act of her sublime affection and constancy
but a few grim old married wardens and
officials and a poor middle-aged clergyman,
on whom the beauty of her fine form is
entirely lost, as in the stillness of death
she is suspended for a few moments between the cold earth and the far, far sky
to which her noble spirit has fled.

"There is a letter for you, Mrs Spillett,"
said Harrison, as he threw one down on
the breakfast-table in the housekeeper's
room, and then departed to lay the rest on
the hall table before the Colonel came
down.

Spillett opened the letter, and took out

another that was enclosed, which she
hastily thrust into her pocket, to avoid the
inquisitive eye of Jenkins, who silently
entered to get her breakfast. As soon as
she had finished her meal, Spillett caught
up some work from the sofa of state—now
her rightful property if she chose to claim
it—and started off for her young mistress's
room. The Colonel had a great objection
to the servants passing through the hall to
go to Mary's rooms, but Spillett always
went that way if she could, partly from
perversity, and partly because it was a
short cut, so she went that way now.
The Colonel had had a restless night.
He was unhappy about "his child," notwithstanding his faith in Paris, and had
come down earlier than usual to carry his
restlessness into the garden. Spillett no
sooner got into the hall than she heard the

Colonel's well-known step on the stairs, when she flew through the hall and shot up the east stairs without being seen.

The Colonel had the great happiness of having little anxiety about his correspondence, and although he insisted on his letters being on the hall table when he came down, he rarely ever looked at them until after breakfast. "Stow that away comfortably, and you are fit for anything," was his theory and practice. So, without stopping to examine them, he put on his hat, and taking up his stick went towards the hall door. Then he suddenly turned back and went to the drawing-room to fetch a pamphlet on the treatment of vines, he had been reading the evening before, to give to the gardener. On the mat, at the foot of the east stairs, was a letter—a white, sharply defined object on the dark rug.

He stooped and picked it up. It was in a man's big handwriting, addressed to Mary, and sealed with the crest of a hawk and the letters F. W. underneath. He recognised the crest immediately, and with the initials there could be no doubt from whom it came. With fierce indignation he hurried off to his own room and locked the door. "Was he justified in opening it?" Certainly; Mary was a minor and he was responsible for her. Besides, she was deceiving him after all, and corresponding with this fellow—and he tore the letter open without further hesitation, too angry to consider whether it would not have been better to give her the letter and trust to her truthfulness for an explanation.

"The Little Sack, Friday, 4.30.

"I have just heard that you start for Paris on Monday; I well know what that means. You are to be kept away until you have learnt to forget me. Mary! if you still love me as I do you, you will come and meet me for a few moments in the park to-morrow. I will go to that big avenue which runs up from the road to the house. No one will see me, I shall keep behind the trees until you come. I shall go early, and remain all day until you come. You *cannot* refuse me now, we may never meet again. Your grandfather is quite wrong. He is simply ridiculous, and most unjust and wicked to separate us now, after we have been allowed to meet and care for each other. But I will never change to you, and I entreat you to come and meet me to-morrow. If you don't come, I shall not know what to think. I only know I would see all my relations anywhere

first before I would give you up. I shall
go *early*.

"In great haste,

"F. W.

"I can think of nothing but your dear
face as you stood on the stairs in your
garden ; but how cruel you were to me !"

The Colonel's wrath burnt with all the
fire of outraged dignity and authority,
fanned by an undercurrent of self-condem-
nation. He flung his hat and stick on the
table, and walked about the room crushing
the letter in his hand. Then, with the
necessity for immediate action belonging
to a fiery nature, he rang his bell violently.
His first impulse was to order his horse
and go over at once to the Little Sack and
horsewhip "this impudent cub of Satan ; "

but when Harrison, who had come himself on hearing this most unusual summons, arrived at the door and found it locked, the act of having to go to the door and unlock it, brought him to a sense of the irreparable scandal he was on the point of letting loose, and the wrong of handing over Mary's good name to the merciless tongue of the wicked world. Any private suffering of outrage was better than that! So he ordered Harrison to bring his breakfast into his room, and to tell Miss Doddingstead to read prayers, as he was busy.

Harrison saw the Colonel's letters still lying on the hall table, and he had a short time before seen Spillett with a strange look in her face, rushing about and inquiring if any one had picked up a letter, and the truth flashed upon him at once that it was

something to do with Miss Mary. He had
been much puzzled on the return from the
visit to Gloucestershire, by the letters
which Spillett received in a gentleman's
handwriting, and he observed to his wife,
that " Jenny Spillett must have picked up
a very smart follower down there, but
he hoped it was all right "—meaning to
keep an eye on her, and give her father a
hint, as " those letters, he was pretty sure,
didn't come from any one in her position."
The correspondence ceasing, however—as
it was his habit to always receive the
letters when they arrived—he let the
matter pass. But here was another letter
in the same handwriting, which he did not
doubt Spillett had dropped, and the Colonel
had found, and there was a look of trouble
in the Colonel's face that wasn't there for
Spillett. " That letter was for Miss Mary !

and he should have it out with young Madam Jenny directly."

Spillett had not told Mary of the lost letter. She was firmly convinced that Nancy had picked it up, and kept it back to spite her, as she had found her dusting in the hall when she went down again to look for it, and she still hoped to obtain its possession, although Nancy had stoutly denied having seen anything of it.

Mary wondered much that her grandfather did not appear, but Miss Doddingstead was certain " he was making his will, and sorting his papers ; he always did before he went away for any time.

John, when he took the Colonel's breakfast, received orders that " the Colonel would be glad to see Miss Mary in his room for a moment after breakfast."

" I told you so, Mary ; it's something

about the property," said her aunt. "But I don't want him to think too much about me, mind. You must keep up the family and marry. I should do very well with just enough. If anything should ever happen to your grandfather, I should like to go and live at Brighton, its more cheerful than Dover ; just a nice little house, is all I want, and then you and your husband could come over and see me—and perhaps bring the children. But you must not call any of them Augusta. It's an ugly name, and we have had quite enough of it in the family.

"But I am sure I should, dear Aunt Augusta, to remember you," said Mary, colouring, embarrassed, and amused at this future cut out for her, and touched by the real goodness that lay at the bottom of this half-developed character.

"Well, don't be too particular. That is the fault I made; and I am sorry for it now. A woman is best married, after all. It brings trouble, I know, but it's something to live for. But when you come of age, and get your mother's fortune, you must not forget that men are greedy after money."

Mary went to her grandfather's room with much doubt. She did not believe it was anything about the property. He would not consult her about matters of that kind, as he never did any one; and she knocked at his door with some agitation.

"Come in!" said the Colonel with sternness in his voice, and Mary entered.

He was still walking about the room with his hands behind his back, and a mixture of pain and anger in his face. He turned upon her at once.

"What do you mean, young madam, by

disobeying my orders, and keeping up an intercourse with this fellow? I flattered myself that I could trust you, and that you had too much respect for me and for yourself, after what I had expressed on the subject—but I find I have been utterly deceived."

"But, grandpapa! I have neither seen nor written to Captain Wyldeman since I spoke to you the other evening!"

"But I have got his impudent familiar letter, which he sent to you this morning, here in my pocket," said the Colonel, putting his hand mechanically on the breast of his coat. "How could he have known so quickly that we are going to Paris on Monday, if you had not written or sent him word? I gave strict orders to Harrison that it was not to be mentioned out of the house."

"Indeed, grandpapa, I never wrote to him, nor sent him any message about it."

"But, then, how did he come to know it?"

Mary said faintly, "she did not know."

"Then, perhaps, you can't tell me either how this fellow's letter got into the house this morning, or how you came to have assignations with him in your garden?"

Mary was silent. She would not betray Spillett, and her good sense told her it was better her grandfather should be angry and unjust with her, than have a real cause of complaint against her lover.

"Exactly what I thought," said the Colonel. "You are pretending to be very meek and submissive, and all the time deceiving me. Mary! I would never have believed that a child of my race could have been guilty of such conduct."

"Grandpapa, you are most *unjust!*" said Mary, beginning to lose patience, and some of the fire of her "race" coming into her eyes.

"Precisely," said the Colonel, taking the word as referring to his refusal to accept her lover. "That is the exact word applied to me by this impudent pushing fellow in his letter to you this morning," and his eyes glowed fiercely under his dark brows. "He has neither the feelings nor the conduct of a gentleman to take advantage of a girl of your age to force himself upon her family. I will never believe he is one whit more honourable, in reality, than the rest of his disreputable relations. He is quite unworthy of you, and the sooner you forget him the better."

"Grandpapa," said Mary, her eyes and brows having a strange miniature resemblance to her grandfather at this moment, "you are most *wicked* to say so ! He is as good and honourable as you are. I will not hear a word against him, and I will never marry any one else as long as I live ! "

She clenched her hands and stood to her full height before him.

"Go to your room, miss! You forget who you are speaking to. ' Wicked !' that is another of his fine terms this fellow has taught you to apply to me. I order you not to leave the house nor send any letter out of it, or I will shut you up in a convent; and if that whelp of a bad kennel comes near the place again, I will have him thrashed off by the stable men ! "

"You need not trouble yourself about that, grandpapa; he is much too considerate for my feelings to come here when he thinks he is not wanted!" said Mary, with a look of defiance and with generous pride in her lover.

"Considerate! why he is waiting for you in the beech avenue now at this moment! If it were not for the regard I have for my own name and yours, I would go out and horsewhip him on the spot!"

The Colonel looked so terrible, that poor Mary turned and fled to her room, with anger and despair and a crushing sense of injustice at her heart.

# CHAPTER VII.

## THE COLONEL ENTERS A YOUNG LADY'S BED-ROOM AT A HIGHLY IMPROPER HOUR.

THAT afternoon Miss Doddingstead was alone in the drawing-room at half-past five, with the tea-table before her, making superhuman efforts to understand Carlyle's "French Revolution," the only book about Paris she could find in the house.

"It's worse than Bradshaw," she thought as she gave it up, and poured herself out some tea.

The Colonel had been out riding all the day. He had many matters to attend to before he left home, but he had given special orders to Harrison before going out, one of which was to pack his summer things. Mary had not appeared at luncheon.

"Have you seen Miss Mary, ma'am?" said Spillett, coming into the drawing-room as Miss Doddingstead was finishing her second cup of tea, and speaking with the most natural air possible. "I want to know if her fur cloak is to be packed, or if she will take it with her?"

"Oh, she will take it with her I should think, Spillett. No, I have not seen her. Why?"

"Because she has not come into her rooms since luncheon, ma'am."

"What's that you say?" said the Colonel, entering to search for the unusual solace of a cup of tea.

"Miss Mary has not come into her rooms

since luncheon, sir," said Spillett, looking him steadily in the face.

"The devil!" said the Colonel, glancing very sharply at her, then checking himself. "She must be in the house somewhere."

"No, sir, no one has seen her," said Spillett without flinching.

The Colonel was taken very much aback, and he glanced again at Spillett, who stood her ground with an air of delightful innocence.

"But where did she go?" said the Colonel.

"I didn't ask, sir. Do you think she has gone over to the Rectory, ma'am?" she said, turning to Miss Doddingstead to escape the Colonel's eye. This artful bait took, and the idea was immediately seized.

"Very likely," thought the Colonel. "That fellow Maxstead has always spoilt her, and she has gone over to him with this miserable story." "Send over at once and see if she is there, and say I wish her to return home immediately," he said, his wrath again rising.

Spillett escaped with almost too great precipitancy. There was a little want of finish sometimes about this great artist. (This was the fault of her short fingers, which went straight to the object, and troubled themselves less about the smaller matters.)

John soon returned from the Rectory. "Miss Mary had not been seen there."

The Colonel was aghast.

"Had she gone off with that fellow after all?" "Go up yourself, Augusta, and see," he said; "perhaps she is in her garden."

Her father seemed so strange in his manner, that even Miss Doddingstead was moved, and wondered if Mary and her grandfather had had a disagreement about the will. She set off at once for Mary's rooms, thinking as she went up the stairs "that money was hateful, it only led to quarrels; but Mary shouldn't be so strong-headed about things — her grandfather knew best."

She had not gone very far before the Colonel overtook her—his anxiety was too great to allow him to remain in a state of inaction. He felt in his heart at that moment, if he could only find her safely at home, he could forgive her everything, almost to letting her have her own way about "this fellow."

They found Spillett in Mary's room, tranquilly packing her things, but there was no sight of Mary herself.

"Is she down in her garden?" asked he Colonel.

" I don't think so, sir," answered Spillett.
But the Colonel was determined to see for
himself.

" Go away, you old fool! Whoop!"
cried Solomon, not forgetting his cus-
tomary salutation to a departing guest,
as the Colonel and his daughter left the
room.

The Colonel winced; " but she might
keep a kangaroo, if he could only find her
safely at home."

Spillett opened the door at the top of
the stairs, and lighted them down the
steps. Miss Doddingstead stopped half-
way, it being too dark to gratify her
curiosity about the animals. The Colonel
went to the bottom and shouted " Mary!"
Then he called out to Spillett to get a
lantern, " she might have fainted, or anything." Spillett soon returned with Mary's

lantern, and lighted the Colonel round the garden.

Miss Doddingstead descended also, and looked about her at the cages and the goat-house, and all the other strange possessions of her niece. But nothing of their owner was to be seen.

The Colonel returned upstairs. His face was white and looked so terrible, that Spillett, for the first time in her life, was a little afraid of him.

" Has she taken anything with her, Spillett ? " he said, looking at her with suspicion.

" No, sir, not that I know of, except her hat with the little red feather, and her jacket that she wears every day—I don't see them anywhere. Perhaps she has gone to some of the cottages, to say good-bye to her poor people."

Spillett was determined to end this close inquisition as soon as possible; the Colonel seemed to be much sharper than she gave him credit for.

"Very likely," said the Colonel, hope again reviving, "I never thought of that; they keep her talking by the hour sometimes. She will be in soon, I dare say;" and he went downstairs with his daughter, trying to console himself with the thought that she was too sensible after all to commit the wild act he had feared.

Seven o'clock, however, arrived, but there were no signs of Mary, and the Colonel was terribly uneasy. John was sent off again to see if she was at any of the cottages. Dinner was put off, and then a short time afterwards was ordered again to come in. The Colonel had not dressed himself as usual, and could remain nowhere for more than a few minutes together. John did not return until after eight.

" He had been round to all the cottages as far as the new ones at Chalkstead, but Miss Mary hadn't been to any of them since last Monday."

The Colonel's barometer again went down to heavy storm.

" Order the brougham," he said, " and tell Mr. Spillett to drive."

He had eaten very little dinner, but drank more wine than Harrison had ever seen him do in his life before.

Not a word did he say to his daughter on what he suspected, nor where he was going, so that she at last began to get anxious also; but she dare not question him.

" Mr. Spillett had gone over to see Mr.

Croucher about the straw, and had the key of the harness-room in his pocket, but William had been sent to look for him."

"That infernal straw!" muttered the Colonel.

There was always a difficulty and a rumpus about straw at the Manor. Apparently it was the most precious commodity on the face of the earth, to judge from its extreme scarcity and the fight there was to obtain a sufficient supply. It was some time after nine before the brougham arrived at the door. Spillett had left Mr. Croucher's, and had gone on somewhere else to beg and coax for a little of the precious straw.

"Straight on!" said the Colonel, as he got into the brougham without any further directions.

Mr. Spillett was lost in astonishment at

this late expedition. The Colonel never went to a ball, and if he had been going to one now he would have taken Miss Mary. At last he decided it must be some magistrate affair, and he whipped up his horses with decision. It might be some one dying.

"The Little Sack!" said the Colonel, putting his head out of the window when they arrived at a crossing.

As they drove along his reflections were very bitter. They burnt inwardly on himself and also flew outwards in rage towards that "impudent scoundrel." He severely blamed his own want of judgment and self-command in having disclosed that her lover was waiting for her. He did not doubt she had stolen out to meet him, and had been persuaded to elope on the spot. The Little Sack had an evil reputation for

affairs of gallantry. A respectable girl
even had been carried off from her friends
not long since, and concealed there under
their nose while they were hunting far
afield. This fellow might have taken the
hint. At any rate, he should discover if
he had gone off also. If he did not find
Mary there, he did not doubt he should
find a trace of some kind.

Mr. Spillett thought something must
have happened to Captain Huntingcroft.
He must have had an accident in the field.
He had heard that he rode at everything,
as if he didn't value his neck a horse's
shoe ; but he was an uncommon nice young
gentleman of the right good old sort, who
had a pleasant word for everybody without
fear of being thought small of on that
account—very different from some of the
the other sort who thought it the correct

thing to be stiff and stuck up, and he should be very sorry if it was anything serious. But he wondered he had not heard of his being down there again ; and he spun the brougham along through the narrow roads at such a pace that the Colonel, although he liked fast driving at all times, and particularly in his present mood, and always had the " best horses about," wondered, amongst his other troubles, if that fellow Croucher, who was too fond of his bottle, was leading Spillett into following his example. But Mr. Spillett was a first-rate whip, who could trust to the quickness of his eye and hand in almost any emergency, and they dashed up safely at last to the garden gate of the Little Sack.

The Colonel got out and entered the garden which surrounded the house. All was in darkness, and not a sign of life was to be seen anywhere. He then knocked at the door, waited, and knocked again, much louder; but still no answer. Then he stepped back and looked up at the windows. Then he attacked the knocker vigorously again and waited a moment. At last a window opened over his head, and a woman's voice called out sharply, "Who's there?"

"Is that you, Mrs. Crippin? I wish to come in. I am Colonel Doddingstead."

"But I am in bed, sir!"

"Never mind your being in bed. Come down directly; I wish to speak to you."

Colonel Doddingstead was not a person to be denied, even by Mrs. Crippin the redoubtable, so she slammed to the casement, and at length appeared with a light, as the Colonel was beginning to knock

again.   He had not reflected that half a
dozen lovers might have escaped in the
time.   In his eager honesty he thought of
nothing but getting into the house.

"Where is Captain Wyldeman?" he
said.

"He went away all of a hurry, sir, this
evening, and took most of his things."

"Was any one with him?"

"Not that I know of, sir."

"Are you sure he is not in the house?"

Mrs. Crippin thought the Colonel was
out of his senses, to come there at this
time of night and talk like that; and she
remained silent.

"I must come in, Mrs. Crippin, and see
for myself."

"Well I never!" said this embodiment
of sour obstinacy that only another native
of East Kent had any chance of getting

the better of; and she held her place in the door without moving an inch.

"Do you hear what I say, Mrs. Crippin? I wish to enter and see for myself. You forget that I am a magistrate."

Mrs. Crippin had never had any practise in stiffening her back against a magistrate, and she was taken at a disadvantage.

"Well, sir," she said, after considering a moment, "it's not for me to say no to my betters, and I suppose you must do as you please." And she ungraciously allowed him to pass, observing, "But you'll find no one."

"Show me a light, Mrs. Crippin," said the Colonel. And he proceeded to open the door of the room to the left, which he knew was the sitting-room, gun-room, card-room, and smoking-room, of the sporting gentlemen who took the Little Sack.

Mrs. Crippin followed him with surly submission. There was no one in the gun-room, and the fire was out. The Colonel then crossed over to the little dining-room on the other side. That was empty also, and had no signs of immediate occupation. "I must go upstairs," said the Colonel; and he went into the two bedrooms and dressing-room, which were over the rooms below. They were empty, nor did the beds look disturbed, though in one of the rooms some heavy boots and gentleman's things still remained.

The Colonel began to think Mary had certainly not been brought there; but as he knew that lovers were artful, and that a young lady had been successfully concealed there before, he was determined to see every corner of the house. His determination was also heightened by opposi-

tion; as Mrs. Crippin lighted him about
with extreme unwillingness, and with an
air as if she grudged every fraction of a
farthing of the cost of the candle she was
burning for his benefit. He then proceeded
to the door of a room at the back. This
was Mrs. Crippin's own bower, and she
endeavoured to resist his entering; but he
bid her stand back and went into the room,
followed by his unwilling hostess. There
could be no doubt about that room. Those
gowns hanging up against the wall could
belong to no other human being but Mrs.
Crippin herself. He then proceeded to the
door opposite. Here she opposed her
sturdy square figure, and declared it was
quite impossible he could enter there. It
was her niece, Mary Tumber's room; and
she was in bed. But the Colonel had an
advantage over his adversary, as his

obstinacy had the additional quality—not often found with pure obstinacy, so often confounded with determination—of a fine imperious temper; and he ordered her to stand on one side in such a tone that she instinctively obeyed. He then knocked at the door. Receiving no answer, he knocked again, and then entered in time to see Miss Tumber springing into bed. Mrs. Crippin followed him in, and he was able to assure himself that the round red face staring at him over the sheets was not that of Miss Mary Doddingstead. There was another room at the back, which the Colonel also looked into; but it contained nothing but boxes and tins, apples, onions, and ropes, and a petticoat hung up to dry.

The Colonel went downstairs and examined the kitchen and back premises, and then the large stables and coach house, the loft, and men's rooms on the other side of the yard. Then he walked round the house, remembering the hiding-places at the Manor, to assure himself that the structure outside corresponded with that within. He returned again to the house, and proceeded to question Mrs. Crippin, who began to be alarmed lest " that fine-looking young gentleman " had been doing something very wrong, to have a magistrate come searching like that for him in the middle of the night; and she became more subdued and even communicative, hoping to hear something in return.

" He had been out all day nearly, and then he came in all of a hurry, and sent for Mr. Trigg's fly, and had gone to Merton station; and it was as much as she and Mary Tumber could do to pack his things together in time; and he left no orders, and said he would write; and she hoped nothing was wrong, as he seemed a real nice gentleman, and never made a fuss about his eating like the others, and he was always——"

The Colonel cut short this testimonial to our hero's domestic virtues, and, making a brief apology in his grandest manner for having been obliged to " disturb her and Miss Tumber at such an unseasonable hour," he went back to the carriage, and ordered the wondering Mr. Spillett to drive to Merton station.

It is a matter of mild surprise sometimes to outsiders, to find on arriving at a small country station an entire change of officials —they are no doubt " promoted," but from whence are those " promoted," who take their place ? This is what happened to the

Colonel, who seldom used the Merton station.

The Colonel at first could find no one. After a time he unearthed a porter asleep with a pipe in his mouth, in a species of lamp-room, and then the station master was brought out—a patient and forbearing being, like most of our station masters —to the credit of that sorely tried race be it said.

The Colonel made himself known ; which did not, however, produce any marked impression on the unlocalized official mind.

" At 5.25 there was an up train, and at 5.32 there was a down train," he said. " Both stopped at Merton. On Saturday nights there were many passengers going and coming both ways."

Neither the porter nor the station

master had noticed any one in particular, except Mr. Brown of the Dairy Maid and Rising Sun, and Mr. Peartree of Sheppey Grange, who had gone to Canterbury; but the station master thought it was a young gentleman and lady, who took firsts for town; and there was one gentleman who took first for Canterbury, besides Mr. Peartree, and one lady—he remembered that, as he seldom had more than one or two firsts, and often not that. Had the young lady a red feather in her hat? He didn't notice.

The porter said, "There *was* a young lady with a red feather in her hat; and he thought it might have been her who got into the train for Canterbury, but he wasn't quite certain, as the two trains came in nearly together, and he had to look sharp."

The Colonel was in an agony with this conflicting evidence. He did not doubt they had gone from here, but which way? He decided it must be the young couple who had taken first-class tickets for London.

" When is the next train for town ?" he said.

" There is no train for London to-night, sir; the last went at 9.15," said the station master. " And there is no train before eight to-morrow — it's Sunday. There is a train for Canterbury at 11.5, but you won't get on from there to-night, sir."

The Colonel saw there was nothing to be done but to return home. He first thought he would drive to town, but it was of no use arriving in the middle of the night. He did so little travelling, it never occurred to him to telegraph to Canterbury for a special, or he would certainly have done so. He got into the brougham and ordered Spillett to drive home.

# CHAPTER VIII.

THE honest old Colonel had a very bad night. In steering quietly what he thought was the usual course, he had shipwrecked all his happiness by not keeping a good look out ahead, and in losing his self-command at the moment of supreme danger. The bell of Don Carlos reminded him again and again through the wakeful night of the happiness and self-respect that had gone in one crash. He had been so fond and proud of Mary, who resembled in beauty and sweetness of disposition his early lost wife, to whose memory he had ever been faithful. He would gladly join her now, could he go back again over the last few months of his life. When he rose, as he did early, he looked ten years older than he had done on the previous morning.

Breakfast and the carriage had been ordered over night in time for the early train to town. Harrison himself came to know if he meant to return the same day. The Colonel could not say; but Harrison had better have some things put up. The latter, after glancing at his master, said quietly—

" Would you like me to go with you, sir ? "

The Colonel thought, " Certainly not, he could manage perfectly by himself."

Harrison persisted quietly. " They could do very well without him for a short time, and he had been thinking of asking for leave to go to town and see his nephew, who was a sergeant in the police, and stationed at Scotland Yard."

The Colonel seized the idea. Harrison was a clever fellow, and discreet, and he would take him into his confidence—glad of something definite to steer for in his restless voyage of discovery.

"Very well, then," he said, and Harrison departed to give John orders, and attend to his own affairs; but before the Colonel came down to breakfast he put a few drops of ignatia into the bottom of his tea cup. He then had a hasty conference with Spillett, and declared he would not have the Colonel killed for any one, and insisted on certain orders he gave being carried out if they did not return the same day— giving her the address of the hotel the Colonel always went to in Jermyn Street.

The Colonel and Harrison soon started, and in due course of time were on their way to town. Whether it was the marvellous effects of the ignatia, said by the disciples of homœopathy to be so wonderful in its rapid effects on mental distress accompanied by self-mortification, or whether it was the distraction of a cheerful and talkative acquaintance in the train, the Colonel certainly looked more himself when they arrived at Victoria. Harrison thought it was the former, and that, with the aid of his little bottles he should pull him safely through even this great trial. But Harrison was an enthusiast.

On arriving in Jermyn Street, the Colonel briefly told Harrison the circumstances of Mary's "unfortunate attachment and its lamentable consequences," and that he had ascertained they had come to town together the evening before, and that he must go at once and find a detective to trace them from their arrival. Harrison said, with the Colonel's permission, he would go and find his nephew at Scotland Yard, and ascertain the proper steps to be taken to get one. The Colonel assented, and in the mean time he would try to find Captain Huntingcroft, and see if he knew where they were. So he started in a hansom for that purpose.

On arriving at the barracks, the Colonel sent up his card to the Hon. Dick, who was comfortably at breakfast in his rooms.

" Wyldeman's done it, I'll bet a pony ! " he said, getting up in haste. " But why the devil didn't he give me notice ? I shan't know *what* to say ! " He gave orders for the Colonel to be admitted, and rushed into his bedroom to put on a proper coat.

" Are you aware of what has happened, Captain Huntingcroft?" said the Colonel, coming in with a hasty step. "That fellow—that friend of yours—has eloped with my granddaughter!"

" Impossible!" said the Hon. Dick, with an air of innocent astonishment.

" But I tell you it is a fact. They came to town together last night. Have you heard anything of them?"

" Nothing whatever, Colonel," said the Hon. Dick, with a look of great concern. " Won't you sit down ?—I suppose you have had breakfast?" And then he began to feel rather sorry for the distress of the old man.

" But have you no idea where they are likely to have gone?"

" Positively none—unless they are gone to Paris."

" I think, Captain Huntingcroft, you are

not altogether without blame in this matter; and I call upon you to assist me to find them at once."

"They must be married now, Colonel Doddingstead—if they are not married by this time already."

The Colonel looked very blank, and sat down. He had felt this must be the final result, if Mary's good name was to be saved.

"You may be quite sure that Wyldeman will do everything that is right, and that her honour is perfectly safe in his hands."

"Honour, indeed—to steal away a child of her age!"

"But then, don't you think, Colonel, they ought not to have been allowed to come together, if you had such an objection to the match? He is a gentleman, and a good fellow, and will have a good property.

You must pardon me if I say I think you are not quite just to him."

" Captain Huntingcroft, I have already expressed to you my insuperable objection to this marriage ; and we will not, I think, discuss that any further."

The Hon. Dick remained silent.

" Why did you allow him to have the Little Sack ? " said the Colonel, feeling a necessity of attacking somebody.

" Wyldeman is one of my oldest friends, Colonel. We were at Eton together, and he was so desperately gone on your grand-daughter, I could hardly refuse him. Besides, I expressed to you openly my sympathy with the marriage."

" It would have been much better, sir, if you had not interfered in the matter at all. But we are wasting time; the question is, will you help me to find them ? "

" With all my heart, Colonel Doddingstead, if I can ; but I have little more idea
where they are gone than you have."

" You mentioned Paris. What makes
you think they may be gone there ? "

" Because Wyldeman has an uncle living
there who swears by him ; and I shouldn't
be surprised if he has taken her to his
house. But don't you think, now the thing
is done—don't you think, sir, it would be
better to wait until you hear from them ? "

" I must assure myself that they are
properly married—if it must be. I must
confess I have not the same confidence in
the man that you have."

The Hon. Dick reflected a moment. " It
would be better to let the old man work
off his steam by hunting for them ; he
couldn't do any harm now."

" I will telegraph, if you like, to his

uncle. I know him very well, and have stayed in his house. He will tell me if he is there, I think, if I say 'important.' He knows we are sworn friends, and they won't know I have seen you. If they are gone there they would have taken the mail last night. Let me see," he said, taking up Bradshaw. Yes, they could do it easily, I think. What time did you say they left?"

" Between five and six," said the Colonel.

" Yes, that's it. By changing at Canterbury, they might have caught the night mail which leaves Dover at 10.5, and they would be comfortably there by this time. I will telegraph at once. But it's that confounded Sunday! We may have a bother."

The Colonel assented, though he was convinced in his own mind they came to town last night; and it was agreed he should go back to his hotel and wait until he heard from the Hon. Dick.

On arriving, he found Harrison waiting for him with a quiet and even mild-looking individual, with none of the received outward signs of either courage, strength, or great intelligence. He might have been a respectable butler out of place, a city clerk, or even a country solicitor of small practice. This was the famous detective, Sergeant Johnson, more dreaded by the "profession" than all the other detectives put together. With a very few questions, he obtained the information he wanted. But the Colonel could give no description of our hero, as he had never seen him. His father was dark and tall—he would probably be dark also, and they could have had no luggage.

Sergeant Johnson said that was no indication at a town station.

" At least the lady had none, but the gentleman had," said the Colonel.

That was a very distinct intimation, the sergeant thought. He smiled a little at the small red feather.

The Colonel had a brilliant idea; he might get a photograph of Wyldeman from his friend. The sergeant said photographs, unless they were taken specially for the force, with the hands shown, were very deceptive. He had found they had as often led him astray as not, except it was hunting any one down at close quarters, when yo had time to study their face. Porters and cabmen weren't to be trusted a bit to go by a photograph. What he wanted was a precise description—tall or short, dark or fair, or any

particularity of dress and manner.    But it
was more difficult to fix young gentlemen
than any one—they all looked at first sight
as if they had the same tailor and the
same hatter.

The Colonel said he would send a note
at once to Captain Huntingcroft.  Sergeant
Johnson said he would go meanwhile to
Victoria and London Bridge.  The lady
having no luggage was almost enough for
him.    Porters were very sharp in noticing
luggage, much more than they did the
people it belonged to—and a young lady's
luggage was very different from a gentleman's.    But Sunday was a bad day, as half
the porters were away.

The Colonel then wrote a note to the
Hon. Dick, and sent it by Harrison, and
Sergeant Johnson went off to Victoria.

The Colonel walked up and down the

room with short turns, very much like the bear at the Zoological Gardens, and in much the same humour. The Sunday before Mary was seated quietly by his side.

"Who would have dreamt of such a thing happening! He would see they were properly married, and so forth; but he would never see her again. She had grossly deceived him, she had acted like an intriguing maid-servant! It was lamentable! lamentable! And he had thought her so truthful and high-principled, and with such a right sense of her position. But it was all the fault of that impudent scoundrel — he had bewitched her. What was to be expected of the son of such a father? He had been only too right in opposing the marriage."

At length the Hon. Dick arrived. He

had received a telegram from Paris; it contained the simple word "No."

The Colonel was now more convinced than ever they were in London, and as he shared the popular delusion of the super-human faculties of a detective, he did not doubt they would soon be found.

Harrison had arrived some time since, with a description of our hero as given by his admiring friend, which the Colonel had read with astonishment, it was so unlike the idea he had formed of him—" Very tall and well made, with broad shoulders, bright blue eyes, fair hair and long moustache, fresh healthy complexion, with a particularly honest and open expression, and a cheery voice and manner; quietly but well dressed, and a rather quick way of walking."

Sergeant Johnson now appeared again.

He had found no trace of the fugitives either at Victoria or London Bridge; and he must wait until to-morrow, when the regular porters would be on duty. Neither had the cabmen given him any information which he considered " close."

The Hon. Dick pitied the state of the old Colonel, alone in an hotel, with nothing to do but to think of his trouble. He thought it would be much better for him to return home.

"No more can be done at present, Colonel. Don't you think you had better go back to Whitepatch, and leave it to us? You might leave your man, he seems a sharp fellow, and, to tell you the truth, I would rather not have one of those detective fellows continually after me at the barracks. Besides, he might go with the detective to recognize your granddaughter, if he thinks he has found them. I assure you I will do everything I can, and let you know at once."

But the Colonel declared he would not return home until they were fouud.

" But it is by no means certain they are in town. They may have stopped on the way, or perhaps are somewhere much nearer home than you think. I am almost certain, if Wyldeman had brought her to town, I should have heard something from him by this time. He knows I am on his side. We might hunt for them here, you know, and you might search about down there. You may get a letter from her there to-morrow morning."

The Colonel thought he might depend upon Harrison, who he knew was devoted to Mary, to see that she was really looked for ; and then he might get a letter which would be delayed if he remained; so he finally consented to return home and institute inquiries in the neighbourhood, if they were not found to-morrow in town, and he had heard nothing from Mary.

The Hon. Dick accompanied the Colonel to the station, Harrison mounting outside. On the way the Colonel was silent for a short time. Then he suddenly burst out—

" But there are no settlements! and my granddaughter will have a very good fortune of her own when she comes of age, which will be entirely at this fellow's disposal."

" Colonel Doddingstead, I will be answerable for Wyldeman that he will do everything that is right and usual in these matters, precisely as if he had married her with your consent. He is a most liberal fellow, and although he has much too small an opinion of himself—which is really about his only fault—he can put down his foot when he is driven to it, and hold his own with his father in a matter of this kind. If you will allow me to say so, Colonel, it will not be long before you come round to my opinion that your charming granddaughter will have a husband as worthy of her as any fellow can be, and that any one might be proud of—all the women are after him, too; and it is wonderful that he has kept so straight. I am afraid I should not have done so if I had had his chances!"

The Colonel was much comforted by these assurances; and more particularly by the genuine manner of the Hon. Dick, which carried conviction more than his words; and, with his loyal nature to those who belonged to him, he began to feel even disposed to take his new grandson-in-law's part against any one who should object to him. Harrison, before the Colonel got into the train, begged him to have the kindness to deliver a note he had written to Jenny Spillett about something in the house-keeping he had forgotten to tell her. The Hon. Dick started at the name of Jenny Spillett. The Colonel put the letter unsuspectingly into his pocket, and said "he would give it to her after prayers,—he would not forget."

# CHAPTER IX.

THE following day at Whitepatch passed
quietly. The Colonel, on his return the
evening before, had informed his daughter
of "the calamity which had occurred."
She had been lost in a sea of conjectures as
to what could have happened to Mary, but
had never once suspected the real truth ;
and further, she had been tormented by the
burning curiosity of Jenkins, who would
not be convinced that her mistress knew
" nothing whatever about it."

After breakfast Miss Doddingstead con-

stituted herself an amateur detective, and
went up to Mary's room to see if she could
find a letter or anything that could throw
light on her whereabouts, secretly revelling
in the freedom of entrance to such a
forbidden ground. Jenkins would have
given up the luxury of abusing Spillett for
a whole month to accompany her; but her
mistress was too much afraid of Spillett to
venture to take her. She found that young
person with a calm face seated at work in
Mary's sitting-room. She rose as Miss Doddingstead entered, but there was a look of
mischief in her eyes as she turned to put
down her work.

Miss Doddingstead had been ordered by
her father to "hold her tongue and say
nothing for the present;" but he might as
well have shouted to the weather-cock over
Don Carlos to keep stationary.

" It's very sad, Spillett," she said, in a low confidential voice, as if Mary was lying dangerously ill in the next room.

" Dreadful, ma'am ! " said Spillett in the same tone.

" But where can she be gone, Spillett ? "

" Perhaps she has had a quarrel with the Colonel, and gone off to Lady Worthingham's for a bit, ma'am. She is staying in London now. Miss Mary had a letter from her the other day."

" It is not that, Spillett, I must tell you, but you must not say a word to any one about it—she has gone off with a gentleman ! " she said in a loud whisper.

" I'll never believe that, ma'am ! "

" But it's quite true. The Colonel knows all about it. He knows the train they went by, and he went to London yesterday to find them, but he could hear nothing ; but they will soon be found, as the head of the detectives is looking for them."

"I am sure it is some mistake, ma'am. Miss Mary knows better than that, and you will see."

Spillett's bold spirit enjoyed skimming on the edge of a danger, particularly when she had to encounter dull wits.

"You don't know anything about it, Spillett. He came here on Saturday, and carried her off from the Beech Avenue."

"If that's true, he is bolder than most men, ma'am. But I would never have believed any man in these days had spirit enough in him for that."

"Do you think she has left any letter or anything by which we can find out where she has gone?"

"I don't think so, ma'am."

Solomon was deeply silent. Miss Doddingstead's whisperings were something new, and he listened intently.

"I should like to see," and Miss Doddingstead proceeded to rummage.

She then went into the bedroom, but she could find nothing but Mary's ordinary correspondence, nor any place that seemed locked up. After she had satisfied her curiosity by an examination of all Mary's effects, she said, "I think I will go and have a look at the garden, Spillett;" on which this active young woman opened the door at the top of the stairs.

After carefully examining everything below, and being much disappointed at not finding the rats, which Jenkins had assured her were there somewhere, and thinking it very shocking to put up a tombstone like that over a parrot, she came upstairs again, and went to her own room to write to one or two of her friends.

But Spillett could not resist the temptation when she was gone of dancing up to Solomon every time she passed his cage, and saying in Miss Doddingstead's voice, " She is gone off with a gentleman."

The Colonel passed the day anxiously, every minute hoping to get a telegram. He answered his business letters, scarcely knowing what he was about, and committing himself to accepting a terrible radical as a tenant to one of his farms by leaving out the word " not." Still no telegram arrived. At length, as he was sitting down to dinner, John, who, having been left in command had assumed an air of importance, handed him one with extra state and ceremony, dimly conscious there was a movement in the air which required extra manners—a funeral was the model which presented itself to John's mind. The Colonel opened it in haste.

" No trace has been found," was the brief information it contained.

He handed it to his daughter, and continued his dinner in silence, and nothing more happened until evening prayers. He then stayed up until after midnight in his room, smoking the great pipe.

He passed in review Mary's life, her birth, and the death of her mother immediately afterwards—followed not long after by the death of her father, who, having little confidence in the wisdom of his sister, had entreated his father to watch over his little Mary. He thought of her earnest activity as a child; her affectionate and sensitive disposition; the first lesson he had given her in riding, and her first fall

on the sands when her pony shied at a
sudden wave. Her passionate anger and
grief at being separated from her doll,
which was suspected of having mineral
poison in its beautiful complexion ; the
coming of Miss Van Tromp and Mary's
obedience to her, and her quickness and
application in learning ; then her dangerous
illness, her quick recovery, and her rapid
growth into a young woman. He especially
remembered her charming appearance at
the ball, and the general admiration she
had excited,—and it had all ended in this—
a runaway marriage, which, however, it
terminated, would loose the slippery tongue
of scandal never to be completely silenced,
even to the third or fourth generation !

At length he decided to go to bed, and
lit his candle. On going into the hall, the
great silence of the house suddenly re-

minded him that he had forgotten to wind up Don Carlos—Monday being the day for that important event.   He returned to his room, and lighting a German silver lantern, with a strong reflector, which he had had in his possession for years, he proceeded to the east stairs, which led to the clock tower. It has been mentioned before that the doors on this staircase were seldom closed ; and the picture of Margaret Doddingstead at the top could be seen when standing at the bottom near the drawing-room door.   On arriving at the foot of the stairs, the Colonel threw his light upwards, and proceeded to mount.   He had gone up only a few steps when he saw something quickly descending the upper flight.   It paused an instant on the middle landing, and he saw distinctly for the first time the Maiden of the East Stairs.   She looked at him with a bright smile, and then rapidly went up the side stairs towards the door of the Quixote room.

He stood for a moment transfixed with astonishment. Could it possibly be Mary herself—it was her look and expression—or was it the famous maiden he had so often heard of from a boy?

He mounted resolutely up the stairs to the door of the Quixote room. It was locked outside. He turned the key and looked in, but there was nothing but the furniture, and the solemn bed done up in brown holland. He then tried the other doors, but they were all locked, and he returned, wondering deeply.

He had never seen one of the ghosts in the house before, and had always obstinately refused to believe in them, though he had acted about the one in the library as if he did.

He returned to the hall, and blowing out his lantern, he took up his candle and went to bed, entirely forgetting his clock. He thought over all he had heard of the history and traditions of this maiden and her appearances. His father and grandfather had both seen her, as well as others. Do what he would, it was impossible to quite believe that every one could have the same delusion and see the same thing. The maiden, he was sure, was a good spirit; she brought harm to no one, and gave warning of danger. But that one in the old dairy, ah! if there was any truth in it, that was the spirit of a devil. It was well known to his grandfather that Van Goyen had shot a man in cold blood whom he knew to be innocent, to appear zealous to the government. And that was why the smugglers murdered him—and serve him right too!

He must search and see if his bones were really in the chalk hole, they brought ill-luck to the house. It was odd he should have that too. No one else had skeletons. And the one in the library! Ah! he didn't know! But he had been wicked to punish Mary for the bad deeds of her lover's relatives, when his own family at one time had been violent and doing every-thing that was bad short of absolute murder, and he was not sure even about that. His grandfather told ugly stories of what he had heard one night when he had had too much wine. It was that, perhaps, after all, which had made him so keen about the Wyldemans' misdoings, and not real honesty. He had been well punished. But the maiden had smiled—that meant well; she had not smiled to his father when his sister Augusta was married, and that marriage was bad enough for anything. She had looked at his father in a way he had remembered for long afterwards. No, he felt happy about it now, Mary—— And he went off to sleep, and dreamed that Mary came to his bedside and put her hand on him with her old happy smile, and that he was lying in the Don Quixote room.

The Colonel had a good night, and awoke much refreshed, and John's solemn announcement that the clock had stopped again was received with equanimity.

On the hall table he found a letter addressed to him in Mary's handwriting, with the Charing Cross postmark. He opened it calmly. "Huntingcroft was right; it would all turn out as he said." He felt resigned to make the best of what could not be helped, and even to be content. "Women were such fools about marriage, it might have been worse." There was no date or address.

" DEAR GRANDPAPA,

"Do not be unhappy about me, as I am quite safe and well taken care of by kind friends who will allow no harm to come to me. I have not seen Captain Wyldeman since I last saw you, nor do I intend to see him, and you must not think it is anything of that kind. But you have hurt me *so much* by what you said about him, and so long as you think like that— which I can hardly believe you really meant—I could not see you and be dutiful to you as I ought; and it would kill me to feel again the terrible pain I had when we last met. Indeed, dear grandpapa, you do him *very great* wrong, and it is not his fault that he loves me so much. Why was I allowed to see him every day for so long a time, if he is so wicked and not a gentleman, as you say? But I do not believe it—I never will. My own heart tells me he is good and true, and it is a *shame* for the world to make him answerable for his relations' faults. I have given him my faithful promise, and indeed, indeed, I will never marry any one else now. I will not marry him without your consent—that I feel would be wrong and wicked, and I should never expect to be truly happy if I did. I could not before God promise to be obedient to my husband with such disobedience to you on my conscience. I have quite made up my mind, if you do not love me enough to give your consent, I shall become a Sister of Mercy and live always amongst the poor.

"Thank you for all your goodness and

love to me. It almost breaks my heart to do this, but I feel that it must be so now, and that it is for the best in the end; but forgive me, dearest grandpapa, for all the pain I have caused you.

"Your still loving and dutiful granddaughter,

"MARY DODDINGSTEAD.

"P.S. Dearest grandpapa, do not be uneasy about me. I am *quite* safe and well taken care of. I entreat you to give your consent; if you do not, I feel that I shall never, never, be truly happy any more."

Again was the Colonel thrown violently off his balance. He had made up his mind to accept the marriage, but now his old prejudice against it rebounded with new force from the reaction.

"Sister of Mercy, indeed! That came of

her reading all those idiotic books, and corresponding and sending money to those busybody women who can never remain quiet in their natural position, but must be doing something to astonish the world and torment their relations ! She must be found at once and brought home. A child like that to be persuaded to give up her rightful position in the world — and to settle whom she will marry before she had seen anything of life! It was monstrous ! She could marry whom she pleased, with her beauty and fortune and position—and to have the matter settled offhand like this ! It was simply ridiculous and absurd ! "

He did not give himself time to note the firmness and plea for justice, or the tone of steady deep feeling that was in her letter, or the earnest appeal at the end. He took in the leading facts only, and treated the rest as girlish nonsense.

"It was just a larger doll being taken away from her over again. But she must be found."

He put the letter into his pocket, and went out into the garden to consider what was to be done. She could not be with Lady Worthingham, as he knew she was only a short time in town on her way to Nice, and must have started long before this. He caught at the idea of the Sisters of Mercy. Mary had been much interested in a charming book published by one of these ladies, and had written to the authoress and sent her money for her work; and a correspondence had been carried on for a short time which he had not at all approved of, though there was nothing in it he could object to reasonably. Was she gone to this lady? He could remember neither her names nor address. His daughter or Jenny Spillett would know. He would telegraph at once to Harrison to go there. It was somewhere near London — he remembered that; and he entered for prayers with anything but Christian feelings in his heart towards those " busybody women and their new-fangled notions of justice and mercy."

After prayers, he informed his daughter of what he had heard and his conjectures; but he kept the letter in his pocket. Miss Doddingstead could not tell him the address of the institution to which Mary had sent money.

" Of course not," muttered the Colonel. " Never mind, I'll find out for myself."

Immediately after breakfast he went straight up to Mary's rooms. No one was there but Solomon, cracking seeds in his cage. He soon found among her books and pamphlets one with the address he required, and he was writing it down on a piece of paper when he heard a strange whisper that sounded like his daughter's voice. "She has gone off with a gentleman!"

He started, and was more alarmed than he had been by the apparition of the night before. There was no one in the room. Was this another ghost? He became quite nervous, expecting something to appear, when his eyes fell upon the parrot. Could it possibly be that ill-bred mountebank? But where had he caught that phrase so quickly? That was certainly Augusta's voice. She had been talking then, and that sharp brute had heard her. Never mind! he should be more careful in future. He was an idiot to suppose that she could keep anything to herself. But it was very annoying. The tale would get about. He must make up his mind, however, to the stories that Mary's folly would set going, and he returned down-stairs and sent a telegram to Harrison. He then went to wind up Don Carlos, frightening Miss Doddingstead by the terrible look he cast on her when he met her in the hall as she was returning from a hasty confab with Jenkins.

In the course of the day the following telegram arrived from Harrison. "Been to institution mentioned; nothing seen or heard of person wanted. Sergeant John-son been to Dover; no trace found."

The Colonel then sent another telegram. "All the institutions of the Sisters of Mercy to be visited at once. Sergeant

Johnson to find out all there were in the country, and go to them."

The Colonel, however, had had a severe lesson. " He would do nothing harsh or violent, not even use his lawful authority to the utmost—-but he would not have her turned into a Sister of Mercy."

Before luncheon time it had been known, as far as the stables and the Rectory, that Miss Mary had become a nun.

John Spillett was greatly moved, but said he did not believe a word of it, " lies bred faster than rabbits." He tried to get some real explanation from his daughter of Mary's disappearance, as he was certain she knew; but he was defeated by that astute young person at every point. She knew quite well he would regard the matter from the parent point of view, and was as likely as not to consider it his duty

to inform the Colonel, fond as he was of
Mary.

The day passed and no fresh news of
any kind arrived. Then a week passed.
Telegrams and letters came, but no trace
of Mary could be found. Many religious
institutions had been visited by the in-
defatigable Sergeant Johnson, and many
excellent ladies had been disturbed without any results. Neither could anything he heard of Captain Wyldeman.
The Hon. Dick had used every effort to
find him, and had written twice to the
Colonel on the subject. Sergeant Johnson
confided to Harrison that it was his opinion
she was hid away with her young gentleman somewhere all the time, and that if
they could only get a clue to him they
would find her fast enough ; if not, it was
some friend who was hiding her up to

starve the old gentleman out. He had
wanted very much to go down to Whitepatch himself, but the Colonel would not
hear of it. He regarded a detective as
something uncanny that was better kept
at a respectable distance.

" Then he won't find her," said the
sergeant; " it's nearly always like that with
people. They often treat one of us as if we
were spies or newspaper reporters, instead
of treating us as friends who want to help
them—as if it wasn't for our own credit's
sake! I am getting very tired of the
whole business! They pretend to think
me too good to take me out of the active
line and promote me, though there are
others quite as good and better than I am.
I shall retire when I get the first chance.
If I could be down there for only a day or
so, I feel almost certain I could find her.

There is generally a little something if you know where to look for it. I do half my business by sitting down and thinking about it, instead of rushing off here and there to see. Sometimes it flashes upon me in an instant, when perhaps I am only thinking about finding a clean shirt; but that's what I call laying the train. Your mind goes on working all the time without any buckling up on your part."

Harrison recommended him to take pulsatilla; he was too sensitive, and took things too much to heart, and he offered to give him some.

Sergeant Johnson examined the little bottles with great curiosity. " He had heard of homœopathy. What was it?" Harrison said " it was using a needle instead of the kitchen poker to go into a very small place."

The sergeant, with all his genius, did not seize the analogy.

"You see," said Harrison, " we are made much more delicately than any watch that ever was turned out as a curiosity. Well now, if a watch is wrong you don't go and set it to rights with a sledge hammer—you use the most delicate tools you can get. All that chemist and druggist business is sledge hammering, and these little medicines are fine tools so delicate that you can't find or taste anything in them.'

"But you don't mean to tell me they can have any effect? I should be sorry to have my beer made in that fashion. I like my beer to be pretty strong, and my medicine too when I want it."

"No effect!" said the enthusiast, warming up. "Look at that little bottle there— that's got a most delicate medicine, made

from a serpent's poison, that will rouse
a man or an animal up at the point of
death. I have seen it myself. It's well
known to the experiment men—the big
fellows who really know, there is nothing
to be found in a serpent's poison, or tasted,
except a little gum; and yet that will kill
a man in half a day. Do you mean to tell
me, sergeant, that any medicine that ever
was made can have less found in it than
that?"

Sergeant Johnson was carried out of his
habitual depth. Those sort of principles
wouldn't go far in collaring a criminal, and
he did not continue the argument. Harrison gave him some little globules screwed
up in a piece of paper, with instructions
how to take them. The sergeant put them
in his waistcoat pocket, but it is much to
be doubted if they ever went any further.

# CHAPTER X.

### THE HON. DICK IS TEMPTED BY FOUR-YEAR-OLD MUTTON.

THE Colonel was in despair. He was quite convinced, however, that some of those Sisters of Mercy were concealing Mary all the time; and he gave orders that the institutions should be watched, no matter how many people were employed—particularly the one he most suspected. They must climb up somewhere and look into the gardens; Mary would never stay long in a house without getting into the fresh air wherever she was.

"It was monstrous that women who

professed to be so good should do such
things; but they would put it under the
head of 'pious fraud,' he supposed.  A
very convenient phrase, indeed, that could
be stretched to anything!"

The Colonel wrote such doleful and
touching letters to the Hon. Dick, that that
amiable person was moved with compassion.   He would go down to the Little
Sack for a week, and cheer the good old
boy up a little.   He informed the Colonel
of his intentions, and was at once invited
to come to the Manor, the Colonel saying he could put up his horses, too, if he
liked.

The Hon. Dick reflected a moment, held
back by his habitual dread of being bored.
But no, the old Colonel, although he was
rather an oddity, was not a bore.  He
would be left to amuse himself pretty

much as he liked; and then he should be very well "done" at Whitepatch in a good old-fashioned way. That four-year-old mutton was superb, and hardly to be got anywhere except at his father's, and the wine was just right (the Hon. Dick was a good judge of wine, and had a delicate stomach which suffered many things from the ignorance of friends on this subtle matter, and, as his father was extremely rich, owning half a county of coal and iron, he had always been able to "do himself" extremely well). Yes, he would accept the invitation.

On the following day he arrived with his man Finch, a very smart gentleman's gentleman indeed, much more got up than his master (who, for a Guardsman, cared little about his dress), and a professional flirt of the first water in his own society. The

Hon. Dick found himself very comfortable.
A saddle of that "delightful mutton" in
prime condition appeared at dinner, and
the wine was even better than he thought
it was, on tasting it quietly again. He
shied rather at family prayers in the evening. But it was nice and old-fashioned,
and seemed to go with the house; still he
thought he should have to miss it in the
morning—"one didn't feel cheerful enough
at that time of day to be reminded of all
one's sins."

The housekeeper at the Manor did not
appear that evening.

The Hon. Dick found himself the next
morning in the dining-room before the
servants came in to prayers without exactly meaning it. The young housekeeper
came in at the head of the servants, but
she had an unusually bright colour in her

face, and he stared at her earnestly as he stood behind the Colonel. At breakfast he said little for some time. The Colonel talked politics, but as his guest was a strong amateur Radical he held his tongue, not wishing " to shock the old man."

Captain Huntingcroft was slightly but well built, and rather above the middle height; about thirty years of age; with soft dark hair and small dark moustache; a small well-shaped head, not much developed over the brows, but well developed in the organs of comparison, benevolence, and imagination; he had handsome and expressive dark gray eyes, a clear pale brown complexion, and a very kind expression free from conceit.

" May I ask, Colonel," at length he said, " who was that young lady person who came in at the head of the servants to prayers? She reminds me very much of some one I have seen before."

"Oh, that's Jenny Spillett, the house-keeper—a wonderful girl for her age," said the Colonel, going on to relate her history, and the history of her family.

The Hon. Dick listened with great interest, but was silent and thoughtful. After breakfast, he said, "I think I shall keep quiet this morning, Colonel, but I should like to go down into the little garden with the high portico, and make a sketch of that white goat if I may be allowed—that is, if it is still here."

The Colonel, a little wondering, said, "Certainly, the goat was still there he believed, but wouldn't he find it too cold?"

"I am used to that," said his young friend.

"I will show you the way, then," he said, " when you are ready."

" No, please don't trouble yourself, Colonel. I know the way. I have been down there twice before with—when I was here last time."

The Colonel sighed softly to himself, and then presently said, " Very well, only don't get a chill."

The Hon. Dick was an excellent amateur artist of the sketchy first-impression order, and could draw figures if not with great correctness or much individuality, yet with spirit, resemblance, and quickness. He went for his drawing materials and his cigar case, and putting on a warm great-coat, he started for the little garden, meeting no one on the way. Although he was strongly tempted to peep into Mary's room as he passed, he refrained.

On getting down below he seated himself a moment in the little summer-house, and lighted a cigar. He thought about Mary and what "a charmingly natural girl she was." He could have been very fond of her if there had been no one else in the way; but he had got over that now. He was not such an ass as to go on thinking about a girl who was turned inside out about another fellow. Then he surveyed the garden, and laughed as he thought of his friend's adventures there. That was the door by which he had escaped. By Jove! he would make a sketch of the place. It would be great fun to show it to them and chaff about it afterwards. And the old brick walls, and the raised brick doorway, and the lines of the garden, he also thought, came very well. "He would do it;" and he set to work. Then, as he

was drawing away with that half-attention
so often given by those who have not to
earn their bread by it, he thought again
of the young housekeeper. "It must be
she or her sister, though she was much
changed in appearance. But there could
not be two Jenny Spilletts. Was it a
cousin. No; it must be she. How very
odd! How was it he had not seen her
when he was down here before or heard
her name?"

There was a light active step over his
head. Some one came down the stairs
almost at a bound, and the subject of
his thoughts passed close before him.
"Jenny! then it is you!" he said, starting
up and offering to shake hands with her.

Spillett had a bright sudden blush in
her face, but she did not shake hands with
him. "Yes, sir; but didn't you know I

was living with Miss Mary now ? I never thought to find you down here in the garden."

"Not an idea of it. She only talked about you as her 'maid Spillett;' but she never called you Jenny, and I thought it was a much older person."

Spillett laughed. "Perhaps it would be much better for me, sir, if I was."

"No, you are charming as you are— more charming than ever!"

"I thought, sir, you had promised never to talk to me—in that way again. If you do, I shall go away directly, and I want to feed all the little animals."

The Hon. Dick put on an air of penitence. "What a little prude you are! I want to hear how it was you left Madame de Gros. Have you seen any of the other girls since you left?"

"Father didn't like my staying there any longer, and I came to live with Miss Mary soon after I saw you last, sir."

"I made inquiries for you, but they told me you had gone into the country to get married; and I was quite jealous."

"Captain Huntingcroft, you are forgetting again!"

"But, Jenny, is it true? Tell me who it is;" and he looked at her with earnestness.

"I am going to feed the Queen of Sheba, sir, and you had better go on with your drawing; but I don't know who gave you leave to come down here," she said, as she went off to the goat-house.

The Hon. Dick followed her. The sight of the goat reminded him of his friend's adventures.

"Then it was you who met Wyldeman

in the lane!" he said, a new light breaking in upon him.

Spillett coloured again, and stooped
down to arrange the goat's affairs.

"But how is it, Jenny, I never saw you
when I was down here before?"

"Perhaps I didn't want to see you,
sir."

"Oh, I should not have said anything."

Spillett was silent, and thought that
even the nicest of men were stupid.

"But where do you think Miss Mary is
gone?"

"I never think about it, sir. She will
come back again when she wants, I dare
say."

"Wyldeman is an idiot. The Colonel is
more dead set against it than ever now.
He ought to have carried her off when he
had the chance."

"With a coach and six horses, sir?" said Spillett archly. "Perhaps she wouldn't let him."

The Hon. Dick wondered a little. That was his own idea, but he had forgotten the exact expression he had used to Mary.

"I can manage that by myself, sir," she said, as he rushed to help her move a box. Their hands touched and their heads were close together.

"Jenny!" he said, standing upright again, "do you know, I did really care a little for you; but I did not find it out entirely, until you were gone."

"So much the worse for you, sir. I mean," she said, colouring again, "that you cared for me at all."

"Why? Then there is some fellow down here, after all, you wish to marry?" he said with a sting of jealousy.

" Perhaps, sir—who knows ? "

" Just like me.  Here I am, poaching again," he thought to himself.  " But tell me one thing : Is it all settled ? "

" I don't mind telling you that, sir.  It's a long way from being settled yet."

The Hon. Dick thought intently for a few moments.

" But I must go now, sir."

" Stay one minute !  I want to make a sketch of you in my drawing."

" But I really can't, sir ; I am house-keeper now, and have a great deal to attend to."

" Just three minutes only ; I am going to give it to Miss Mary."

It was impossible to resist such a pair of handsome eyes, and Spillett allowed her-self to be put into position.

" Where did you get that wonderful old

grandmother comb?" he said, as he looked at her critically.

Spillett made no answer, and he then set to work and rapidly drew in the outline of the figure, and was getting the head well forward when the model became impatient.

"I never knew such a long three minutes, sir, in my life! I really must go, or they will be coming to look for me."

"But will you come again?"

"Not if you talk as you have been doing to-day, sir."

"I *promise* you I won't, if you will only come for *five* minutes, to-morrow."

"Will that be by the same clock as the three minutes, sir?"

"What a girl you are! But I promise it shall not be long, if you will come."

"I don't believe you have been drawing me, sir, after all."

"Look here, then." And he showed her a spirited sketch, well advanced, of a very pretty young woman.

Spillett was mortal. She was highly impressed by such talent and masterly rapidity, and her own appearance in the drawing.

"I will see, sir. Perhaps I will come for a short time," and she darted up the stairs and disappeared.

" By Heavens! I would marry that girl, if she would have me!" he said to himself. "But what would my old governor say? She is a lady by birth, however, after all, it seems. I always thought she looked rather like one. How very odd she and her father should be in such a position! But there is that other fellow she wants to marry. I must try and cut him out this time. I must mind what I am about though, women are the very devil to move if they are once gone on another fellow." And he went on with his drawing, lighting cigar after cigar.

In the afternoon the Hon. Dick became impatient, and got the Colonel out for a long ride. He felt the ground again carefully, to see if there was any chance of his coming round to Mary's marriage. But the Colonel said " he did not wish her to marry until she was of age. A young woman had not completed her education until then. He did not approve of girls marrying too young, for many reasons. They only saw the world in the distance, and they ought to be allowed to get nearer and see things as they really were; and it never answered for a woman to have daughters looking about the same age as herself. If he could find Mary, he would travel for a year or so—there was nothing like travelling for changing people's ideas about everything. He ought to have taken her before. He would never put off such a thing again."

On their return, the Hon. Dick renewed his acquaintance with Mr. Spillett, and studied him more closely. He decided he was anything but a common coachman, and would look very different out of his servant's clothes. The excellent Spillett little thought what was passing through that "nice young gentleman's mind."

The young housekeeper appeared again at prayers that evening, and the Hon. Dick thought that family prayers were not such a "stickler" after all. It was interesting, and had a nice quieting effect, and made one think of going to bed early. It was awful the way one managed to stay up every night about nothing at all; that was why one felt so down in the morning. He would reform; though he thought it would hardly pay to have in Finch and read prayers to him when he wanted to go to bed early.

Mr. Finch, in the mean time, had been using his utmost powers to fascinate Spillett in the housekeeper's room; but he was completely routed, and had to confess to himself he had never met her equal for making a man feel small. He was also greatly taken with the good looks of Ruth at the early dinner in the servants' hall; but as to getting up a flirtation with one of the under servants—that was quite beneath him.

The next morning, the Colonel received a letter from Harrison, with the same old story. Sergeant Johnson also wrote to the Colonel, rather to his surprise. He again urged, on his own account, that he might be allowed to come down to White-patch. Although he did not allude to it, a suspicion had arisen in his mind that Harrison was not particularly anxious the young lady should be found. There was something at the bottom he did not understand. The Colonel suddenly changed his mind about detectives. "They were blundering fellows, after all. He should have to go himself. He was certain those women had got her somewhere or other. What was the good of these fellows if they could not find out? What did Huntingcroft think?"

"Well, Colonel, you know what I think about it; but as matters are, I should let her alone at present. She will get home-sick before long, and want to come back."

The Colonel sent orders to Harrison to

go on watching the institution, but he did not say anything more about going himself, and he obstinately clung to his opinion that she was in London or the neighbourhood.

After breakfast the Hon. Dick escaped from the Colonel as soon as civility would allow, and hastened down to the little garden. He was afraid Miss Jenny would be beforehand with him and feed the animals before he came. He sat down in the summer-house, lit a cigar, and proceeded to spoil his work of the day before. Presently he heard a slight sound over his head; he started out and looked up. "There she was!" He thought he had never seen her look so pretty, or her womanly figure appear to greater advantage, as she stood in that position glancing down at him, and she had a shy look he had never observed in her before.

" Well, are you coming down ? "

" That depends, sir, on how you are going to behave."

" I swear I'll be as good as the old Colonel ! "

Spillett laughed. " Well, sir, I'll come down just for a short time, but I must feed the little animals first." And she descended slowly.

The Hon. Dick would not " go on with his painting." No, he wanted to look at the " little animals " also, and he went round with her. " How could her young mistress be so fond of such little brutes ? They were only fit to be kept in a kennel ! "

" Miss Mary must have something to love and take care of, and the more they were despised by other people the more she seemed to like them," said Spillett.

" I will never believe that parrot was

one hundred and twenty years old," said the Hon. Dick.

" He was over a hundred for certain, sir. Perhaps Mr. Harrison stretched a point to please Miss Mary."

" He must have stretched a good many points, I think."

" No, sir, he's generally pretty correct."

" But, Jenny——"

" I am called Mrs. Spillett now, sir, and I would rather you called me by my right name."

" Well, then, Mrs. Spillett, middle-aged, plain, and most disagreeable housekeeper at Whitepatch Manor, when are you going to retire from your pots and pans and get married ?"

" I am not going to tell you anything more about it, sir; and if you are going to stick me up again like a stone statue in the cold, the sooner you begin the better. It's to be only five minutes, remember, sir. And I shall go by my own watch this time."

The Hon. Dick placed her in position. "I shall talk to you a little, and then it won't seem so long. You mustn't move when I speak, mind. But what have you done with your comb? It was charming, and suited you exactly!"

Jenny neither moved nor answered.

"Tell me something about your family. The Colonel told me a little."

"There isn't much to tell, sir."

"Don't turn round and look at me when I speak!" he said, the enthusiastic artist prevailing over the lover for the moment. "That is all nonsense; where did you live?"

"At Ixstead, sir."

"What! that charming old place near the Little Sack? I made a sketch of that, and have been inside the house."

"Yes, sir; and the Little Sack belonged once to my grandfather also."

"You don't say so! how very odd! Well, but how did you lose it all?"

"I believe my grandfather was really quite mad, and he sold everything to a Jew at Shrimpgate, for nothing at all hardly, they say; and there was some property at Shrimpgate that went with it that's worth I don't know what, now, sir."

"Extraordinary! Well, but now—just move a little this way—not too much; that will do nicely. You are a capital model, Mrs. Spillett. Well, who has got it now?"

"The same family, sir, I believe. They own half Shrimpgate; and most of the public-houses, where the people come down for Saturday and Sunday, belong to them, they say."

" Do you know their name ? "

" If you are particularly anxious to make their acquaintance, sir, I dare say father can tell you; I believe they have turned Christians now."

" No, I have no intention at present of spending either a Sunday or Saturday at Shrimpgate.   But was nothing saved ? "

" Nothing at all, sir, except a few things father has."

" How very odd!   Haven't you any relations ? "

" None hardly in Kent, sir, except very distant ones.   Father and I are the only Spilletts left, except the Spilletts in Dorsetshire, and they wouldn't look at us now."

" Don't be too sure of that.   Have you ever tried them ? "

" Father wouldn't do that, sir; it's the last thing he would do."

The Hon. Dick went on drawing in deep silence.

" It's getting on to half an hour, sir," said the model, glancing at her watch, " and I *must* go; and I can't stand again for you, sir. Some one will be seeing me out of Miss Mary's windows; they come in there now at odd times."

" But you *must*, Jenny!"

" Indeed, I can't, sir; you won't see me down here in the garden again."

The Hon. Dick was silent a short time; then he said suddenly—

" Jenny!—Mrs. Spillett—will you marry me? Don't look round; and don't alter the colour of your face like that!"

" You ought to be ashamed of yourself, sir!"

"Dear Jenny, I am quite serious," he said, pausing in his work and looking at her earnestly. "I have loved you ever since I have known you, and you know it. If you will marry me, I will be so fond of you and so kind to you, that you couldn't help being happy; and I am sure you will make me very happy."

Spillett did not reply immediately.

" Jenny! " he said with soft entreaty.

" No, sir," she said quietly. " I don't think I should make you happy—at least, not in the long run. I know the world a little, young as I am, because I have always been obliged to notice and think a great deal; and I know what fine ladies and gentlemen are. You would have a bad time of it if you married a servant, and had a coachman for a father-in-law."

"Jenny, you are quite wrong! You forget that a man in my position can marry whom he pleases. I should like to see any one snubbing my wife!"

"Not a servant, sir. If I had been an actress that no one could exactly answer for, or even a woman divorced, you might easily enough," she said with some bitterness; "but not a servant. You would never be forgiven that."

"What nonsense, Jenny! Besides, you are a lady by birth."

"Oh, I know, sir; people won't believe that. And there is another thing—well—it's better to speak out the truth plain, sir," a beautiful colour coming again into her face, which had grown pale, "a woman doesn't like to be looked down upon by her—well, sir, her descendants," meaning her own children.

" Jenny, misfortune has not agreed with you. How bitter you are ! "

" Perhaps I may be, sir, because I don't feel like a servant, and yet I am obliged to be one ; and I know father feels the same. It is not the masters and mistresses ; it's the other servants."

" Jenny, if you will marry me, I will let the world go to the devil and take care of itself ! "

" You think that now, sir ; but you wouldn't some day."

" You are as obstinate as the old Colonel and Mrs. Crippin put together ! "

" But I really *must* go, sir ! "

" Jenny, you care for some one else ? You don't care a straw for me ! "

She glanced at him, but he did not catch the look in her eyes, as in his mortification and disappointment he was looking down and mixing up his colours all wrong.

"You have no right to ask that, sir; but I am grateful to you for the honour you pay me, and I will tell you the truth. I have no intention of marrying any one."

"But do you care for me a *little*, then, Jenny? If you and your father were in a better position, would you marry me?"

"You are a very kind gentleman, sir, and one man is pretty much as good as another, and if I were obliged to marry— perhaps—I might. But that can never be, and it is no use talking about it any more. I am going now, sir!"

He caught her in his arms as she tried to escape, and her lips trembled as they met his. She lingered a brief moment, and then tore herself from him and flew up the stairs with a great patch of scarlet vermilion on her shoulder which had run from the colour-box he still held in his hand.

"By Heavens! I believe she cares for me a little, after all, and I'll marry her yet, if the whole world says no! Thank God, there is no other fellow this time!"

Spillett appeared regularly at prayers, and the grandmother comb was again in her hair, but the Hon. Dick could not get sight of her at any other time. He wrote a very touching letter, sealed it, and tied it up to the horns of the Queen of Sheba. The note disappeared, but no answer came to it, nor could he succeed in catching her in the garden again. At the end of his week, he was obliged to return to town on duty.

In the mean time, nothing was heard of Mary or her lover, and the Colonel began to think she was deceiving him worse than ever, and that "the best of women would outdo Ananias and Sapphira for the sake of a lover."

During Mary's disappearance, Spillett paid several visits to Canterbury. "She had to settle her clothes to her new position."

# CHAPTER XI.

## THE RECTOR GOES INTO BATTLE.

During these recent events, the worthy Rector had been at Bath, steeping his rheumatic limbs in that excellent water, and only returned home on the Saturday after the departure of the Hon. Dick, early in that same week. He had heard confused and contradictory reports of what had happened at the Manor during his absence, but he felt certain his obstinate old friend the Colonel would probably prove to be wrong in the misfortune which had happened to such a sensible girl as his granddaughter. He was greatly perplexed in spirit to know what part he should take in the matter, or if it were safe to take any. The Colonel knew the hour he was expected to arrive, and about five o'clock wrote a note to ask him to dinner that evening, if he was not too tired after his journey. Spillett met John coming out with it in his hand, and she had a flash of inspiration. "The old Rector was a bachelor."

"I am going over to the Rectory in a few minutes to see Mrs. Evans, and I'll take it," she said; and John gave her the note.

The Rector was drinking his tea, and looking at his accumulation of letters and papers by the fire after his journey, when his servant came in and said Mrs. Spillett had brought a note from the Colonel, and wished to see him for a moment. The Rector had long known Spillett, and considered her a remarkably intelligent and superior girl, who knew what she was about. He had been very pleased to hear of her promotion; and he was not at all of the opinion of his own housekeeper that such a "mere girl" was much too young for her post. "It was not the age," he said; "it all depended on the person." So the young housekeeper was received graciously, and congratulated on her new position, and so much did they find to say to each other, that the interview lasted nearly three quarters of an hour. After he had sent by Spillett a hasty note to the Colonel, accepting his invitation, he neglected his papers and sat down to think.

"He must brace up his nerves, and act like a man, whatever came of it. It was as he expected. But what a sly little puss! It was as good as a comedy!"

The Rector found his old friend looking much the same as usual after his recent troubles, except that he was a little sad and mournful. " What a tough old fellow he is ! " he thought ; " it would have killed me ! "

The dinner did not commence very gaily. The Colonel said little, and his daughter had not the faintest idea of the art of throwing the ball in general conversation. She could hold forth in a dull way on any-thing that occupied her mind, if any one would listen to her ; otherwise she remained silent. The Rector, however, drank his champagne, and made head against the prevailing stagnation—becoming cheerful and full of his own peculiar quaint little stories and observations on things and persons at Bath. Then the Colonel cheered up a little also, and by the time the two old gentlemen had finished their modest one bottle—Miss Doddingstead never touched champagne; it made her face red, she thought—the dinner went very well indeed, as the Colonel had plenty to say in his own way when he was in the humour, or had any one else to start him.

As soon as Miss Doddingstead had retired, and they were alone after dinner, the Rector brought his courage to the sticking-point and alluded to the "unfortunate trouble" he feared his friend had had during his absence. The Colonel remained silent a moment, and then, hesitating a little, began to relate his misfortunes— finding it a great relief, after all, to have a friendly and, as he believed, sympathetic ear wherein to pour them. The Rector cautiously sounded him as to the strength of his resistance, and found it was, as he feared, almost invincible. The Colonel did not conceal from him the mistake he had made from his over-confidence and want of foresight in the matter of the young people meeting, nor yet the good personal character he had heard of the young man, though he placed small confidence in it himself, " he knew the breed too well." The Rector saw it was hopeless to attack the Colonel in the front, and point out to him the mistake he had made in over-straining his prejudices and authority when the mischief was done; so he made a skilful flank movement. The Colonel had produced Mary's letter, and the Rector called his attention to the firmness of its tone, and the great improbability of a girl of her character changing her determination, now that she had given her promise. He thought it extremely likely she would

carry out her intention of joining one of
the religous institutions, as she had often
talked to him about them. " It was un-
necessary," he said, " to point out to him
the consequences, for if she once did so, his
granddaughter would probably remain un-
married for life, and the Doddingstead
family would come to an end in the
county."

This was a tremendous hit, and shook the
Colonel on his pedestal even more than
the Rector had hoped. The Colonel had
not thought that could be possible. " It
would be too monstrous." He had been
bitterly disappointed by the death of his
son without a male heir, and had built all
his hopes on Mary's marriage. But he
still held his ground. " She was a mere
child. It was absurd to suppose she
would never in time like some one else."

The Rector returned to the charge. " He thought her youth was the worst part of it. His experience of life had shown him that the real shipwreck of women's affections had nearly always come in early life, before they had been tempered and hardened by contact with the world; and the more honest and good they were, the more complete was the catastrophe. A girl of Mary's sincere and earnest nature, who had lived her life of retirement, was a sacrifice bound hand and foot ready for the fire of a false god. It was his honest opinion she was a girl who would never give her heart now to another man, and she would certainly never marry any one to whom she could not give it. He felt certain, also, she would not marry without her grandfather's consent; and it was a million to one if any man would wait for

her until after his death. And then, what a
poor thing her life would be compared to
that of a woman surrounded by her children
—even if her husband was not quite all
that could be desired."

The Colonel sat in deep silence, and a
tear came into his eye. At length he asked
the Rector if he would have any more wine,
and proposed that they should go into the
drawing-room. On going through the hall,
he took his old friend's arm, stumbling
over the little step near the drawing-room
door, which he had known all his life.

The Rector retired early, to "finish his
sermon for to-morrow"—no one was aware
that he had written a new one for many a
long year—and as he walked over to the
Rectory, he thought that matter must be
practically settled, for he had never known
the Colonel let him have the last word on

any subject whatever on which they differed in opinion ; and he decided he should have to get a new surplice for the wedding, as he hung up his hat by the side of his old one.

After the Rector had gone, the Colonel sat in his large chair, glancing alternately at the portraits of his ancestors. He dwelt particularly on an ancient picture, the portrait of Sir Cuffe Doddingstead, the founder of the family prosperity. He had thought it unfortunate enough that the family would at last end in a female representative; but it was worst of all if it should die out altogether. But it was nonsense ! She was a mere girl yet ! Still, that quiet fellow Maxstead was not without a grain of good sense ; and he gloomily recalled the number of times he had proved right in matters on which they had differed in opinion. "He would go to bed, and leave the matter until the morning."

It is necessary to return a moment to the Hon. Dick. Sir John Wyldeman had been failing for some time, and on his return to town, the young Guardsman found himself besieged with letters and telegrams to know what could possibly have become of his friend, as nothing had been heard of him, and Sir John was seriously ill. He advised an immediate insertion in the papers of the fact, and to wait the result. A few days afterwards our hero burst in upon him on his way to Gloucestershire. He had been living in Paris, acting under superior orders to let no one know where he was.

The Hon. Dick shouted so loudly with laughter at a short account of the real state of affairs given him by his friend, that his neighbours came running in to see what was going on.

Wyldeman hurried off to the Great Western, but the Hon. Dick broke out again several times after his departure.

The Colonel, after a restless night, came down the following morning still undetermined. Such a deep-rooted prejudice was not to be torn up at a moment's notice. He went to church, and to the astonishment of his parishioners, the Rector did produce a new sermon, which he had composed at Bath to fill up the long hours in the evening. His more simple hearers would have preferred one of his old ones; they were like so many chapters in the Bible, which they could listen to without fear of what was coming, and without the effort of extra attention. The subject and substance, however, of this new discourse was

as old as the hills.  It was on the blessings
of health and the rewards of a regular and
temperate life, both in this world and the
next.  He had gone over it carefully the
night before, to make sure that not a word
or sentence could be construed into preach-
ing at his old friend in his misfortune, or
offering him advice publicly.  The Rector
always classed the Church of England
under four divisions—the High Church, the
Low Church, the Broad Church, and the
Gentlemanly Church; he prided himself
on belonging to the latter.  Its watchwords
were " No meddling impertinences ; " " No
wrenching of the religious screw."  He
was of opinion that what was not given
willingly to God was of small value.  It
did more harm to the individual by stirring
his anger and hypocrisy and dislike to his
minister and religion, than good to the com-

munity at large. In his sermon he main-
tained that good health was very much a
matter of good sense, a regular life, and a
right appreciation of God's intentions in
the use of ourselves. That religion which
came only from ill health and a fear of
death, was slavish and unwholesome, and
would have a heavy discount at the day
of judgment. God was a God of infinite
jealousy, and would not look with favour
on those who turned to Him from a selfish
fear at the last moment. The perfect
Christian was the healthy soul in the
healthy body, the healthy body being nearer
to the perfection of God than the diseased
one, and also freer from the many tempta-
tions which beset the latter. God set a
model for our guidance in order and regularity in the sun, the moon, the stars, and
the whole universe. He who led an

irregular life, departed from the manifest
intentions of God and could only expect
punishment, for disobeying Him, in ill
health and consequent unhappiness, and
often misfortune. If we had not health,
we had not happiness ; and the honest
labourer, with health, though he might
complain of his lot, was a far happier
man than a duke in his castle without it. The rich man sometimes wondered that the poor man was able to live
on the simple food he obtained ; the poor
man might wonder, with much greater
truth, that the rich man was alive at all
on the excess of food which he took.
(Miss Doddingstead thought of the famous
good dinner she had watched the preacher
eat the night before—the Colonel would
have been horrified if he had known
either the thought or the proceeding—but

Jenkins did not admire either the Rector or his sermons!) If a man had good health and a good conscience, he had every essential requisite that God intended for his earthly happiness, and all beyond was often only a burden and a pain, which lost its value and became little but weariness and vexation as life advanced. The humility which Christ had taught us as the absolute and only true condition of a right faith in Him, was almost impossible for those who deliberately strove for riches and worldly honour. (The Colonel winced a little, and wondered if all that was intended for him. The Rector had not thought that such old common-places of religion could be so taken.) He wound up by exhorting them when they went to their work in the early summer morning amid the dew on the hedgerows, and in the winter through

the pure and beautiful snow on the grass
and fields, and saw the great sun ever
daily starting anew on its journey ; and
when they returned again from their
labour in the evening, and saw it sinking
to its rest in splendour ;—to remember that
it was God's pattern of a daily regularity
that never failed in its appointed task,
bringing health and the beauty of life in its
train. In running, then, their daily course,
let them above all things be orderly and
regular ; let them make their duty to God
and their neighbours a fixed habit of their
lives, and it would then cease to be irk-
some, and come to them as naturally as the
rising and the setting of the sun. Let
them think of the evil that would ensue if
that broke its regular course for one day
only, and never to forget that we were
equally a part of God's creation and that

the same law applied to ourselves. He must remark, in conclusion, that he had always found those who did not come to church regularly, were the most disorderly in their own houses, the least healthy and cleanly, and the least prudent and successful in the management of the simple means which God in His wisdom had given them.

With the exception of Jenkins and her mistress (so called) the Rector was greatly respected and liked in a quiet unconscious manner by his parishioners. All felt it would be a sorry day when he should have to leave them, and all were pleased to see him looking so much better for his sojourn at Bath, as he had lately shown symptoms of declining. But one of his clerical neighbours, who was always at war with his own parish, declared that Maxstead's sole religion was " Come to church, and wear a clean shirt."

# CHAPTER XII.

THE COLONEL DISCOVERS SOME NEW RELA-
TIONS, AND DETERMINES TO FIND A
GOOD HUSBAND FOR JENNY SPILLETT.

In the afternoon the Colonel sat in his
room and looked at his pedigree. He did
not remember ever having done so syste-
matically before. "It was such an affair!"
He had only glanced at it for an occasional
reference. All that sort of thing he took
for granted, and did not lay any undue
stress on his advantages in that way. The
Doddingsteads had held the land for
twenty-five generations; that was enough,
and spoke for itself.

He was much surprised to find, however, that his great-great-grandfather had married one Jean Spillett, of Ixstead. The Spilletts, then, were his cousins; and they had never even alluded to it or presumed on it in any way! He was very glad he had made Jenny housekeeper; he should like to do something for her father. He wondered whether he could set him up in one of his farms. If he could only get rid of that bottle-loving fellow Croucher, he might make him his bailiff and agent; but Croucher did not neglect his business, and did it well, and his private habits were no business of his. He would see about a farm for Spillett.

He then looked again at the interminable list of names and marriages. It was sad that such an unbroken descent should come to an end—"but she was a mere child."

All his arguments with himself ended in this. He locked up his pedigree again, and took down a volume of the history of Kent and turned to the name Spillett. He was again surprised. He knew they were a good old family, without being very great. But he found it was nearly as old as his own; and also, what he had not observed in his own pedigree, a Spillett had married a Doddingstead in the time of Elizabeth, and had descendants—so that his coachman and housekeeper had Dodding-stead blood, and Ralph Spillett, the lover of the unfortunate Margaret, was her own cousin. "It was astonishing, when families got down in the world, how those things slipped out of sight!" But Spillett and his daughter had a great deal of the right sort of unobtrusive pride. He had found that out several times in dealing with the father, and the daughter was himself over again; but they were the sort of people who would get down to be crossing-sweepers, if left to themselves. He must attend to it. He was not sure the daughter ought to remain in service; but it would be a great blow to Mary to part with her. By-and-by he would find her a good husband, and set her up in some way or other. In the mean time he would increase her salary, and she could save. He then read the description of the Spillett coat-of-arms, and, putting down his book, went out into the hall and looked at the window.

He was so familiar with it since a boy, that had he to pass an examination as to the coats which were there, he really could not have said anything for certain about them, except that the Doddingstead coat

with many quarterings was in the centre.
Yes, indeed, there was the Spillett coat,
and a very good one too—simple, like all
the good old coats. How very curious
that he should not have known! He
wished he had known before, Huntingcroft
seemed taken with the Spilletts. He would
have been interested to hear what he had
discovered.

At this moment that impetuous young
gentleman was returning by an afternoon
train from Shrimpgate; having, after all,
passed the whole of a Saturday and part
of a Sunday at that cheerful if not highly
aristocratic watering-place.

The Colonel again passed a restless night;
and he almost swore at his old friend Don
Carlos, who persistently returned again and
again to remind him with the same eternal
deliberation of the mess he had made for

himself; and he thought his old repeater in
the watch-pocket near his head had a most
irritating loudness of tick. He would
change it for the Queen Anne that was in
his room below. Those idiotic housemaids,
too, must have been altering the arrangements of his blankets, they were smothering him to death. Jenny Spillett, with all
her cleverness, didn't know how to look
after his bed like Mrs. Harrison. Then he
quarrelled with his pillow; he was certain
they had changed it. His head seemed to
sink into nothing. His bones must be getting thin and sharp, he felt them so plainly.
It was a mistake to live too long. The
weariness of the flesh gets the better of you,
and a man becomes like an old purse with
the framework coming through.

He however came down in time to take
his walk before breakfast, and entered for

prayers as usual, giving more attention
than was his wont to the words he was
reading, soothed by the fine rhythm and
sublime language of the old collects and
prayers for the morning which he had
selected in preference to Bishop Lexicon's,
who had seemed to him of late vapid and
artificial by comparison, without the sympathetic elevation a man wants in times of
trouble. Those men, he thought, were in-
spired, and wrote in times of trouble ; how
could a modern bishop, in clover and fine
linen, feel like them ?

Miss Doddingstead opened the morning
paper. She seldom read anything but the
murders and accidents, and the births,
deaths, and marriages.

The Colonel was standing with his back
to the fire caressing the fine head of old
Shot, still thinking of his trouble, and that

the old dog might last him out yet, when his daughter exclaimed—

" Papa, Sir John Wyldeman is dead ! "

The Colonel snatched the paper from her hand. " Yes, it was true ! " He then threw it away, and sat down to his breakfast.

The matter of " to be or not to be " had been so nicely balancing in his mind, that the death of Sir John sent the scale down on Mary's side, and for a few brief minutes he decided " it should be, and that Mary should be made happy in her own way."

Miss Doddingstead picked up the paper from the floor, and proceeded to look over its contents. Presently she again exclaimed, " Papa, here is a long notice of Sir John."

The Colonel once more snatched the paper from her hand, and read the notice.

In this Sir John Wyldeman was extolled

as a model of all county gentlemanly excellence and virtue ; his amiable and social qualities, his great services in the Liberal cause, and the loss which his death would occasion, were dwelt upon at some length.

"It is all a d——d lie!" cried the Colonel. He crunched the paper in his hand and flung it contemptuously on the floor.

Again did the scale in which poor Mary was placed kick the beam. The Colonel went on furiously eating his breakfast, muttering to himself and twisting his piece of toast savagely in two as if it were the neck of an enemy.

"It is all a d——d lie! Infernal humbug! Plausible scoundrel! Find me endorsing that! No, it shall never be! *Let* the family come to an end! But that is all stuff. The girl is a woman, and only eighteen! Liberal cause, indeed! Radicals and Revolutionists! My name shall never be joined to that!"

He rose at length from the table, and pushed back his chair with such impetuous haste that old Shot retreated howling and limping to a corner.

The Colonel stopped a moment to soothe the dog, gave him a chicken bone from the table, and then went out and ordered his horse, to attend to matters on his property—a sure sign with him that his mind was made up.

# CHAPTER XIII.

BEFORE his departure on his last visit the Hon. Dick had twice paid a visit to Ixstead, and finding the house was still to be let, he had entered and gone over it. It was a charming old rambling black and white Kentish house, to which a new wing had been added in the worst taste by the present owner. A great deal of the old furniture and many portraits of the Spillett family still remained there, mixed up with a collection of odds and ends, old and new of all kinds, until the fine old drawing-room looked like a broker's shop or a sale

room. He had ascertained the size and
extent of the property from the people in
charge, and found that it was a good
property, though not very large. The
house was well placed amidst old trees,
with a distant view of the sea and the
world-known white cliffs. He also discovered it had been offered for sale not
long since, and he determined on the spur
of the moment to buy it. If the Spilletts
would not accept it from him, as a proof
of his love for Jenny, he did not think that
any woman would resist the temptation
of becoming the mistress of the old home
of her family—even if she had to marry
the owner! In any case he would come
down there in the winter to hunt and
continue the siege in a comfortable manner.

On his return to town he rushed off as
soon as he could get away to Shrimpgate;

and by the evening of the same day he had practically concluded what he thought to be a famous bargain with the Christian Jew owner for the Ixstead property—in which he agreed to give a much larger sum than it was worth. But he was an only son, and he was aware his father had a great deal more money than he knew what to do with, and never in the end denied him anything he wanted. Without saying a word to his father, he placed the matter in the hands of the family solicitors, and started off for the midland counties to see him.

After dinner, on the day of his son's arrival, Lord Huntingcroft received the following intelligence.

"I have bought a property down in Kent, sir."

"In Kent! What are you going to do down there, Dick?"

"I mean to slip away there in the winter for a day or two's hunting, when I can manage it; it is by no means good hunting, but I like the people down there and the place. It's awfully healthy, you know, sir. There is sea all round it, and I never feel so well as I do there. But I shall want you to help me a little with the purchase money—if you don't mind?"

"But did you manage it yourself?" said the amiable old gentleman, much astonished at this sudden taste for business in his son.

"It is all in the hands of Heavy and Young, sir, and they'll see I am not done in any way."

His father looked reassured.

"But I ought to tell you there is a woman in the matter also."

"My dear boy, that sort of thing is much better confined to town!" said Lord Hunt-

ingcroft, shocked at the way he thought
his son was going to scandalize the good
people in Kent.   "But why won't you do
what you know I have set my heart on
and marry?"

"But, father, that's it.   It is a woman
I want to marry, if I can only persuade her
to have me."

The old gentleman became highly interested.   "Well, who is she?"

"Well, sir,—at the present moment she
is the housekeeper at Whitepatch."

Lord Huntingcroft turned in his chair,
and stared at his son in amazed bewilder-
ment.

"Housekeeper!   Are you out of your
mind, Dick?"

"No, sir, not in the least; wait till you
hear all about it."   And he related the
history and misfortunes of the Spilletts,

and his intention to reinstate them in their old home if they could be induced to accept his offer.

His father looked glum. He had very different ideas about his son's marriage; but he was too wise to offer open opposition at once.

" But the lady must be old enough to be your mother ? " he said.

" Not at all, father; she is only three and twenty, and wonderfully good looking— bright and fair, like an angel, and awfully clever and nice. But the worst of it is, she won't have me."

" Won't have you ? " said Lord Hunting-croft, more and more perplexed with the whole matter.

" No, sir; she has refused me point-blank, though I am sure she cares for me a little. She swears it won't pay to marry a servant, and that she will not make me happy in the long run."

The young housekeeper rose much higher in the old gentleman's estimation than he thought it prudent to allow.

" At any rate she is not devoid of sense. She is quite right; it wouldn't pay, you may be sure of that," he said.

" But I can't agree with you, father ! " said the Hon. Dick very warmly. " She is good, and she is a lady; now that she is down in the world that is only another reason I should stick to her. But I am really so fond of her I would marry her to-morrow, even if she were nothing but a servant."

" This comes, Richard, of your Radical notions; and I don't know what the family will come to if you go on like this. I suppose the housekeeper is a Radical too ? "

"No, indeed, sir, she is not! She is a red-hot little Tory. We have had many a discussion on that, and she has said more than once she would never marry a Radical, and I shouldn't wonder," said the Hon. Dick reflectively, "if that isn't one of the reasons why she refused me."

"Perhaps—not unlikely," said Lord Huntingcroft, the girl rising more and more in his opinion of her.

"I know this, that if she did marry me, I should have to become a Conservative too, for she is awfully firm about everything. I never knew such a girl for that."

"But would you give up your Radical notions, Dick?" said his father experimentally, rather to sound the strength of his political opinions than thinking of the marriage.

" Certainly, sir! I would do anything in
the world to marry that girl, and to please
you ; " and he added with a sudden, new
impulse, " I would even stand for the
county, as I know you wish."

" On the right side, Dick ? "

" Yes, sir, on any side for that girl—and
you, father."

This was a great bait to Lord Huntingcroft, a keen politician and a staunch Tory
of the old school, who had swallowed much
bitterness in his son's desertion of the old
political faith of the family.

" And you say she is really of a good
family ?   There is no nonsense about
that ? "

" You have got all the old county his-
tories in the library, sir ; I will show you
in three minutes.   It is sure to be there."
He rushed off to the library, and returned

after some time with a large old volume, one of several, of the History of Kent.

Lord Huntingcroft carefully looked at it for himself. "You are sure they are the same family?"

"Not a doubt of it, sir. Colonel Doddingstead knows everything about them, and the property I have just bought is the place where they lived. 'Ixstead,' you see the name there. It is quite close to Whitepatch."

"Well, Dick, I will think about it. We don't want money, and I would give a good deal to see you married and a good Conservative."

The Hon. Dick knew from this he would get his way, "if that obstinate girl wasn't so obstinate!"

On the following morning, Lord Huntingcroft gave his consent on the conditions named, and Heavy and Young were to let him know what they required for the purchase.

After his son's departure, he thought it just as well that " Master Dick should unite himself to such a paragon of firmness and good sense as this girl seemed to be." He did not anticipate any prolonged resistance on the part of the lady, and thought that she showed good judgment of his son's character in putting him to a test of his real feeling; and altogether he formed a high opinion of his proposed daughter-in-law.

## CHAPTER XIV.

THE READER IS TAKEN INTO THE SECRET.

WHEN Mary had her great quarrel with
her grandfather a few Saturdays pre-
viously, she rushed up to her room with
her eyes flaming and her gentle face
burning with anger and indignation.
Spillett was absent, but when she came up
not long afterwards, she seized the occasion
with masterly skill.    It had been her
original intention, if Mary failed again with
her grandfather, to induce her to run away
and hide herself with Mrs. Sherlock at
Canterbury, until " the old gentleman came
to his senses."   She had no very clear idea

of the exact workings of the process, but
she had a full confidence in the result
(again her short fingers). Mrs. Sherlock
had at first consented, readily enough, when
Spillett went over the day before. She knew
the character of her former charge suffi-
ciently well to believe Spillett's confident
opinion that Miss Mary's happiness was
ruined for life, if this marriage was not
allowed to take place; and she knew the
Colonel "took maggots into his head which
nobody could drive out of him." She
accepted Spillett's opinion of men as gospel,
and believed that the young gentleman
in question was in every way suitable for
Miss Mary. But when her quiet little
husband came home before Spillett's departure, he at once put a veto on the matter,
as endangering his position of accountant
at the brewery. The Colonel was a gentle-

man of high position in the county, and the partners of the firm, who had families of their own, would certainly side with him. Spillett had to return home defeated on this point, but by no means discouraged. She had another string to her bow which was even better, though it might not be so pleasant to Miss Mary, and that was to conceal her in the Priest's room over the library—as the Colonel rarely entered that room, excepting when some distinguished visitor was staying in the house.

She told Mary of her discovery, and suggested to her to hide herself there at once, and let the Colonel think what he liked of her disappearance. "That would bring him to book one way or another!"

Mary at first would not entertain the idea of such an underhand proceeding. If she could not now live happily with her grandfather she would like to join the Sisters of Mercy.

Spillett was certain the Colonel would never allow that; he would be even more against it than the other thing. This was her only chance, unless she wished to give up Captain Wyldeman altogether, and never see him again. The Colonel had ordered Mr. Harrison to have all his summer things packed, and on Monday she would be taken away, it might be for several years or even more. Mr. Harrison had just told her of the Colonel's orders. Now that the Colonel had had a good fit of temper over it, he would be more reasonable, particularly if he hadn't any one to stand up and fight him about it any longer, and he would get sorry now for what he had done, and be more disposed to come round.

Mary admitted the truth of this, but it was the idea of being carried off at once for so long that decided her. She was also too deeply stung by her grandfather's injustice to her lover to calmly exert her usual good sense and reason ; so she consented to follow Spillett's advice—" things could not be much worse than they were at this moment."

Mary had also an anxiety about her lover. She feared he and her grandfather might meet ; and men sometimes were so violent, she dreaded to think what might happen. She told Spillett of the information her grandfather had given her, that he was waiting for her in the avenue at that moment. Suppose her grandfather went out to look for him ? Spillett reflected a moment. There was plenty of time. They had the whole day before them. No

one would be likely to come and look for
Mary. So she volunteered to go immediately to warn him and tell him to leave the
neighbourhood at once.

In three quarters of an hour she returned,
with an impassioned note written in pencil
on the half of a letter. "He would do
everything she wished except give her
up," etc. Spillett had found him much
nearer the house than was prudent. He
entered into the plot, and said it was better
that he should go and hide himself somewhere as well—and that would throw them
off the scent altogether. He gave Spillett
the address of an hotel in Paris where she
could write to him, if there was any chance
of his being wanted ; but she was to write
in any case to tell him how her young
mistress was—if she could not persuade
Mary to write herself. He would keep out

of sight during the day, and take a train later, in time to catch the night mail for Dover.

Spillett then boldly locked the door at the top of the stairs leading down to Mary's rooms, lighted a candle, and proceeded with great briskness to show her young mistress the secret passage.

Mary's astonishment was very great that she should never have discovered it, and that no one should ever have known to where that closet led ; she had on several occasions been inside, but so artfully and yet so naturally was the door placed in the corner that she had never noticed it. Her wonder increased when they reached the passage that looked down on the little hall outside the drawing-room door, and Spillett had great difficulty to refrain from laughing out loud when they saw Jenkins and Miss Doddingstead wagging their heads close together in secret conference at the foot of the stairs. But she hurried her young mistress forward, as time was precious for all the arrangements she wished to make that Mary might be comfortable. When Mary reached the Priest's rooms, she was surprised to see their size, and the handsome and even comfortable way in which they had been fitted up. She had imagined from the descriptions she had heard, that they were merely small places in the roof. Spillett had brought with her a sweeping brush, and a good supply of dusters. She opened the window, and the two young women set to work as noiselessly as they could to restore the place to a little order and cleanliness. Finally, they got the place into a more habitable condition. Spillett then decided to light a fire. She pressed

her round young cheek against the chimney-
stack and found it was warm. She was
certain that it was the same chimney as
the one in the Colonel's room, which was
underneath in that part of the house.

"What fun! If the Colonel did but
know when he poked his own fire!"

She then went back and brought coals
and wood. The grate was an excellent old
one, that bowed out with hobs at the side.
It burnt well, and a good fire soon gave
the place a very different look. Then she
brought up some carpets, and a large rug
to nail up over the entrance, and hammer
and nails. The question was the hammering; it might be heard. But she solved
the matter by giving a tap, and then
waiting some time before she gave another
—"that might be the wind or anything."
She then brought up some light pieces

of furniture, books, and Mary's painting materials.

Now about the bed. Spillett said she would bring her own mattress and blankets and sheets. She could manage by taking some from the spare rooms when she had time. They then dragged the bed into a corner, and she threw her plump person down at full length on it to see what it was like, and was surprised to find it almost more comfortable and elastic than a modern one. "She had thought people in those days slept on things like boards."

She brought up some of the tools out of Mary's workshop as fireirons, which did well enough, though Mary thought it was a shame to use them for that purpose. She also brought up a round wooden bonnet-box of her own for the coals; but she found it impossible to coax Mary's bath through the little door in the closet below. She however brought up an empty biscuit tin to stand on the hob for a supply of hot water.

" That's your kitchen boiler, Miss Mary, and you'll have to do most of the cooking yourself, and perhaps some of the cleaning and washing up, as it won't do for me to be out of the way long ; you'll see—Nancy will soon be coming half a dozen times a day now to find me, out of sly curiosity."

Mary smiled. The excitement and novelty of the enterprise and the hope of its success cheered her not a little, and it was also impossible not to be infected by Spillett's air of carrying everything before her. Spillett asked, with her nose in the air, if she would like to have up Poacher, the old weasel. Mary laughed, and said she thought the smell of the cooking would be sufficient; but she sighed when she said, "If the poor king had only been alive!" Spillett said Mr. Harrison was expecting a new monkey to arrive every day; his nephew had heard of a black ring-tail monkey that he thought would do.

"It won't be the same," said Mary.

"You are as obstinate about monkeys as you are about men, Miss Mary," said Spillett.

"I hope friends, too, Jenny."

Her maid threw her arms round her neck, and said she had always known that, and she never meant to leave her for any man in the world; for there was little of the mistress and maid between them now, except the name and the ceremony.

Mary was a little alarmed about the stairs that led up from the old library. Spillett said there was nothing to fear.

The Colonel seldom went to the library now, and never came up into the Priest's rooms, excepting to show them to a visitor. They would watch till he went out some day, and then go down and explore it. This reminded Mary of the apparition that appeared in the library, and she began to be alarmed at the idea of sleeping up there alone.

" I have thought of that, Miss Mary; if you will allow me, I mean to sleep with you. That bed is much bigger than it looks when you get into it."

Mary thought a moment. " No, Spillett, I think you had better not. Grandpapa is very likely to get restless in the night, and come up to my rooms, or even Aunt Augusta and Jenkins. I don't think I shall really be afraid."

Spillett thought it extremely probable

some one would come, and did not press
the matter further. She had also another
feeling at the bottom. When Spillett had
got things a little "ship-shape," she thought
it prudent to make an appearance downstairs. She also wanted to smuggle up
something for Mary to eat. As soon as
Harrison could find Spillett alone, he proceeded to "have it out with her" about
the letter. Spillett promptly took the bull
by the horns, and ended by bringing him
into the plot. She then got her friend
Eliza into a corner, and had little difficulty
in bringing her in also. Eliza hated
Jenkins, who had also "received her very
shabbily" when she took her seat in the
housekeeper's room. Spillett thought by
these means she could secure Mary's comfort
and secrecy.

At tea-time she presented herself in the

drawing-room in the manner before described ; consoling herself for the stories she had to tell by the reflection that all was fair in love and war. In the evening, Eliza and Harrison packed a basket, picnic fashion, with everything they thought Miss Mary could want, and putting in a chicken uncooked, and a small gridiron, according to Spillett's orders, Eliza conveyed it to a cupboard at the top of the back stairs, in the long passage which led to Mary's staircase ; and while the Colonel was sitting in impatient distress over his dinner, his runaway granddaughter was laughingly cooking over his head a " spread eagle," which she ate and enjoyed a great deal more than a distressed, persecuted, and love-sick heroine had any business to do—although it is to be remembered that hunger, love, and distress accommodate themselves to one

another very often in a most obliging
fashion. Spillett had also private instructions to administer to the interesting recluse
several doses a day of our old friend the
ignatia, to be alternated with mercurius if
she seemed restless and unable to bear the
restraint of confinement. Spillett firmly
believed in Homœopathy. Harrison had
cured a sprained ankle for her in almost a
day or so by the administration of arnica
internally alone, which had converted her;
and she dosed Mary without her knowing
it. Mary believed in Harrison, but not in
his Homœopathy.

Spillett stayed up with Mary as long as
she could, and then, having tucked her up,
went down to her own room.

In about an hour Mary awoke in a fright
and heard Don Carlos strike twelve immediately over her head. She counted the

strokes, and thought " it was the fatal hour." The fire was burning low, and a nightlight was feebly shining on the table, which Spillett, with malice intent, had borrowed from Jenkins—" she would feel so lonely up there now Miss Mary was gone."

After a fortnight of bitterly cold weather, the December wind had risen and shook the old roof, howling in the chimney with intermittent bursts which seemed to the excited girl like an unearthly conversation of strange voices in agony and pain. She thought she heard some one repeating a prayer in a low monotonous tone in the little chapel; then a sound as of footsteps on the stairs leading from the library below. She started up in bed, scarcely daring to breathe, and then she thought she heard a voice whisper as if in warning,

"Leave this place." She sprang out of bed, and seizing the light, escaped through the opening into the passage, and made her way rapidly down to the closet, but she found the door was fastened—Spillett having secured it as it would not remain closed of itself, and she feared an early visit from the inquisitive Nancy. Mary began to tremble with cold ; but her natural courage and her young instinct of self-preservation came to her rescue, and calling up all her resolution she determined to return again to her bed. "She had done nothing wicked ; the spirits could not harm her ; God would send good angels to guard her."

On going up the steep narrow steps she trod on her long night dress and stumbled, and her light fell and went out. In an agony she groped her way back until she reached the end of the passage where the stairs mounted again to the Priest's rooms, but she could not find the opening, as the passage went beyond it, and she had not observed that it did so. She could find nothing but a *cul-de-sac*. She thought she had got into some other passage which Spillett had not discovered, and she retraced her steps and got back again to the stairs that went down to the closet; on descending, she trod on the little night-light she had dropped, and then knew where she was. She again returned, and arrived at the same barrier. She now stopped and thought intently. She *must* have made a mistake, and once more she retraced her steps, but only to arrive at the same result.

"Oh, God! what shall I do!" she exclaimed, and she began to tremble violently with cold and fright.

She then thought she would again try the door of the closet. When she arrived there, she pushed with all her strength and tore her nails in trying to open it, but the door opened inwards towards her, and she could not move it either way. Then she drummed with all her might with her clenched hand, and screamed to Spillett with such piercing and agonizing cries that they would have raised every sleeper in an ordinary house, but the solid old walls in that part of the building were as thick and impervious to sound as a dungeon. Her teeth began to chatter, and she felt the cold stealing on her like death. She fell on her knees and prayed earnestly for help. "To be so young and to die like that!" She thought of Margaret Dodding-stead lying dead and white on the seashore. "Was her fate to be the same?" Then she again thought she heard the deep whisper, " Leave this place ! " and she sank in a swoon on the floor.

The robust Jenny Spillett had gone to bed after an unusually hard day's work, and fell quickly into the sleep of the healthy and honest. The December wind increased in violence and drove the frightened rain against her window panes and shook the old house to its foundation. But at length she had a terrible dream. She thought she saw the figure of Margaret Doddingstead lying on the floor, with a face as white as snow, and her wet clothes clinging to her body, and in her hair was the same flower with the two green leaves which she arranged for Miss Mary at the ball. Then the scene changed and she heard a great hammering as of some one knocking in nails, and a voice calling her by name and saying, " Spillett, they are nailing up Miss Mary in her coffin; it's not Margaret Doddingstead—it's Miss Mary."

A violent gust of wind rattled the old casement and the shutters of her window, and she awoke in fright and found her face bathed in tears. She listened a moment to the wind, and then suddenly remembered her young mistress all alone in the secret rooms. What if she should be frightened by the wind! Then she remembered she had fastened the door inside the closet if she should want to come to her. She started out of her bed, struck a light, and putting on a warm wrapper determined to go up and " have a look at her." On trying to open the secret door in the closet she could only move it back a part of the way. She listened, but could hear nothing. She then passed her arm round inside the door and could feel some one there. "It was Miss Mary! She was certain. How wicked and careless she had been! God forgive her, if anything had happened to her!" She put the light down hastily on the floor, and forced the door slowly open until she could get inside, and then she found that it was indeed her young mistress, as cold as ice and stretched on the ground as one dead. But she preserved her presence of mind, and using her great strength, she took her in her arms and brought her into the closet. Then with one hand she placed the light outside in the little hall, and again taking her in her arms, she carried her in and laid her on her own bed. She then ran back for the light, and when she returned, Mary was still lying stiff and rigid without sign of life. The tears burst from Spillett's eyes, and in an agony she stooped down and listened to her heart. She thought certainly she heard it still beating. She dragged the clothes from under Mary, and covered her up warmly. Then she determined she would run and fetch Mr. Harrison. But with an innate sense of propriety even at a moment like this, she rapidly seized the thick mass of fair hair that fell to her knees—which she was always half ashamed of, thinking "it wasn't quite natural for an honest woman"—and tied it up in a knot behind. She was then snatching up the candle to start, when she heard a sigh and a gentle voice saying, "Jenny, is that you? Where am I?"

"Oh, thank God! Then, you are alive, Miss Mary!" she exclaimed, and she fell down on her knees by the bedside and placed her arms around her. "But what has happened to you, dear Miss Mary? Do you feel ill?"

"No," she said, "only very, very cold— but I begin to feel better now. I was only frightened and came down, and the door was fastened, and I could not make you hear" (not a word of reproach!); "and then I don't know what happened."

"Shall I fetch Mr. Harrison, Miss Mary? You may have caught your death of cold."

"No, Jenny, I don't feel ill, only cold and frightened. I think if you would get into bed with me it might warm me."

"You are sure you won't have a little wine or something? I can go down and get it in a minute."

"No, I think I only want warming."

Jenny rapidly got into bed and took her

young mistress in her arms. Her vigorous
life and Mary's youth soon brought a warm
reaction, and after a softened account of
her agonizing adventures, our heroine was
before long breathing softly, and fast
asleep in the arms of her faithful maid.
Mary's hold relaxed gently, but Jenny
remained long awake, tenderly clasping
her as some precious thing she feared to
break by the least movement—a beautiful
expression of protecting love and devotion
in her face. The wind howled and shook
the old house, and blew the candle which
still remained lighted, as she thought what
a crime she had nearly committed in caring
more about defeating her enemy Nancy,
than of safely guarding her " dear Miss
Mary."

Let the curtain be drawn over the
picture of these two young women, each

with a beauty of her own, as they lay locked in each other's arms in the soft light of the flickering candle—so different in appearance and character and yet so alike in the eternal stamp of that womanly goodness and honesty which is the veritable salt of corrupt humanity !

# CHAPTER XV.

## THE RING OF VENUS.

THE expert in palmistry (and they abound to-day) will naturally and very rightly ask, "How do you account, sir, for the tenderness shown at the end of your last chapter by the young person you call your supplementary heroine, who has such short fingers and terrible nails—which generally we believe indicate a want of tenderness and even cruelty?"

"Learned sir, or still more learned madam, I humbly submit that this is a case which shows the extremely intricate nature of palmistry, and the great rashness of judging a character by any one or two even strongly marked indications."

" Then, you are opposed to the dominant indication theory ? "

" Certainly; unless that indication is so absolutely dominant that it has all others in complete subjection to it, as shown in the monstrous ambition indicated by the abnormally long forefinger of Napoleon the Great, or the extraordinary length of the line of the head in a miser, passing nearly round to the back of the hand."

" And pray, sir, when and where did you have the remarkable opportunity of examining the hand of the great Napoleon ? "

" Never. But his well-worn gloves are to be seen any day by those who know where to look for them, in which the general character of the form of his hand is indicated with great clearness."

"But your short-fingered young person, sir?"

"The short-fingered young person in question had other indications in her hand which balanced, and might even outweigh, in certain given circumstances of life, the tendency to cruelty, hardness, and severity shown in her short fingers and nails. She had a very large ball of the thumb (mount of Venus), calm and without lines; and a pure, delicate, unbroken line of Venus in both hands; add to this the double line of life in both hands, which indicates, as you are aware (apart from its great energy and the fortune-telling business), strong sympathy with human nature and active friendliness of disposition, and although, as is evident from the conduct of this young person to her own lover, that her head governed her heart, yet in the left hand the line of the heart was equal in length and clearness to the line of the head and was a beautiful and well-defined line. But as the line of the head in the right hand was longer and straighter than the line of the heart (this being the hand of action and master of life *at the present moment*), it would predominate over the heart in any matter in which her reason was called strongly into play—as in her refusal of the Hon. Dick, though she was in love with him. Hence, this young woman could act with cruelty and even severity should her reason or her enmity be called into action, but also with great tenderness should there be nothing to oppose a free abandonment to the instincts of the heart as shown in the left hand—the love and generosity in the mount of Venus, and the tenderness and passion in the ring of Venus; this

latter, in my opinion, being much misunderstood and belied, indicating in truth a fund
of tenderness and passion in itself, either
in man or woman. It is generally found
in the hand of great genius of the emo-
tional type—dangerous, it is granted, if
broken or in excess—as was most probably
the case in the hand of Byron—but of
supreme value to a gifted nature when
pure, unbroken, and in its right place,
being, in fact, an addition to the line of the
heart which intensifies its qualities for good
or for evil.

Having indulged in this little halt by
the way, the writer again honestly puts
his shoulder to the collar.

Jenny Spillett resolutely kept herself
awake until Don Carlos struck five. She
then gently disengaged herself from Mary,
and proceeded at once to the Priest's rooms.

Having lighted the fire, and put on the kettle, she returned, and stood for a short time beside the bed watching our heroine as she lay with her head on her arm in calm and gentle sleep. At length she stooped down, and with a soft kiss called her by name. Mary awoke at once, much surprised to find herself in Spillett's bed.

"I think you must go back to prison again soon, dear Miss Mary. The Colonel is going to start for London by the first train, and the maids will be up early, and Nancy is as likely as not to come prowling about up here for something. I have got your dressing-gown and slippers, and have lighted a nice fire upstairs and put the kettle on, and I will come up presently and give you some tea. But you had better go to bed again and keep yourself warm. Do you feel all right again this morning?"

" Yes, thank you, dear Jenny ; " and she laughed at her fears of the night before. " But what is grandpapa going to London for ? " she said, a little startled at the news.

" I will tell you all about it when I come up, Miss Mary."

Jenny had kept back her budget of news the night before, fearing to disturb Mary's rest.

Mary then started for her hiding-place, and before long her maid joined her.

" I had to go down and get some cream, Miss Mary ; but there is no one up yet, and we are all safe."

She made some tea and a slice of toast, and when Mary had had her breakfast, she told her of all she had been able to gather of the Colonel's proceedings the night before.

Mary looked very sad, but Jenny

Spillett assured her Harrison would take care of the Colonel, and see that he didn't distress himself too much. He had little medicines that would cure everything— even love! "Would you like to have some, Miss Mary?"

Mary smiled. "Have you tried them, Jenny?"

Her maid coloured a little and said nothing, but she thought how sharp Miss Mary was becoming.

As soon as she had put things a little in order, Jenny went downstairs to attend to her housekeeping duties. She did not return for some time, but when she came up again, she told her the Colonel had just started, taking Mr. Harrison with him, who had declared the Colonel looked so poorly, that he would be quite ill if his mind wasn't quieted a little, and that Mr.

Harrison wanted her to send a letter from
Miss Mary up to him in town by the early
Sunday post, that he could post it for the
Colonel without his knowing where it
came from, to tell him she was safe with
friends, and had not run away with Captain
Wyldeman.

Mary earnestly desired her grandfather
should not think she had eloped with her
lover. As she had no wish to give him
more pain than was necessary, she consented to write the letter suggested. After
a further consultation with Spillett, the
letter we have seen was sent under cover
to Harrison by the early post, which went
at eleven o'clock. Spillett thought it was
safer to go to church, and Mary read the
morning service to herself, and a sermon
by Robertson, her favourite modern divine.

After Mary had cooked her own

luncheon (Spillett determined to keep her to the cooking, though she had declared she could do very well on cold things), her maid proposed, as the Colonel was away, they should try to find the entrance into the library.

But some description of this place must be first given.

In the passage near the Quixote room, and nearly opposite the White Closets' room, was a low, square, solid door which led down by one deep step into the library. On entering, one was struck by its gloomy obscurity, as it was only lighted by one long low window nearly close to the ground at the end by the door to the left. The library was part of the original building, and of the same date as the hall below; its original use could only be guessed at. It had a very low panelled

ceiling, painted in the Italian manner.
The Priest's rooms, which were immediately
overhead, had been afterwards added, and
were of a much later date. The entire
walls were studded with books from floor
to ceiling, in cases with divisions, excepting
at the end of the room, which had a
curious chimneypiece, with cabinets and
drawers for papers on either side of it.
About the middle of the room, on the
right, a partition advanced half-way. This
also was covered with books from floor to
ceiling on both sides and at the end.
In the corner of the room to the left, near
the fire, was a stupendous old square couch
or sofa, considered by its present possessors
to be unique, of quaint structure, and so
large that it would have bedded half a
dozen men at a pinch. At the end of this
couch, near the window, was a ghostly

looking armchair with a stuffed high back, and sides that came forward at the top for the head to rest on, and that looked altogether not unlike a pair of huge shoulders and arms. It was in this chair that the apparition of the old squire sat at dusk, gazing out of the window, with a gun in its hand. A large round table in the centre, and half a dozen heavy old Chippendale chairs completed the furniture of the room.

The mantelpiece was broad, but light in construction, with elaborate Italian carvings, and a long narrow mantelshelf near the top. On seizing this shelf with the two hands and throwing all your weight on it, the mantelpiece descended into the floor about eighteen inches, disclosing at the top a long hollow place in which a man could lie concealed at full length. It received air and light by ingenious contrivances in the carving. This is said to be a virgin hiding-place that was never discovered, and that once had the honour of sheltering a cardinal for nearly twelve hours. In the bay which lies between the half partition and the fireplace, on the right, the entire centre bookcase from floor to ceiling, on being taken hold of by one of the shelves, could be made to slide outwards, and then turned like a door on its hinges. This disclosed a deep closet furnished all round with rows of narrow shelves, which had the appearance of a genuine closet to hold deeds and documents of importance. The walls and shelves of the closet might be pushed and pulled, pressed upwards and downwards, the floor and ceiling examined, and no means of exit but the apparently legitimate one could be discovered, and yet the way to the Priest's rooms from the library was through this closet.

In the upper part of the library window, to the right near the old chair, the following doggerel lines were inscribed. They did not look as if they had been cut with a diamond but rather as if they had been burnt into the glass in the process of making.

" Heir of Whi'puth,
    Wouldst thou for Sorrows sleep no Sorrows wake,
    Thy Troth-Love bring when Gloom ye Dusk doth make;
    Then lingering Joys shall swage my tearless Woes,
    For thy twain Life from hence my Spirit goes.
    Ah! com'st thou not!—as Worm-sought Fruit ye'll die!
    Hand for Hand—O heed! or one from Earth will fly.
                                    " R. D."

This strange and dark inscription had caused much fear and perplexity in the family. According to tradition, it was not

found until some little time after the death
of Richard Doddingstead, who shot his son
from this window. Each generation had
put its own interpretation on the words,
but few had dared to disobey them; and it
had been the general custom for the heir to
present himself in the old library at dusk
with his affianced bride before the marriage
took place. Twice had a marriage been
broken off from the reluctance of the bride
elect to endure and the Doddingstead
obstinacy in exacting the ordeal. The
handwriting was the same as Richard Doddingstead's, as still to be seen in the library
in the fly-leaves of books, and in a small
volume of manuscript poetry written by
him. The Colonel had scoffed at the matter
in his youth as " old woman's stuff," but he
had followed the custom, and taken his
affianced bride there at dusk before his

marriage. The spirit of Richard Dodding-stead appeared to the bride-elect, but the Colonel saw nothing; and when she died early at the birth of her twin children, he attributed it largely to the fright she had received on that occasion, and took a hatred to the place, never allowing his son to enter the room or follow the traditions of the family in this matter. His son and his wife had both died young also, and yet he still clung to his opinion that it was " all rubbish."

Nevertheless, he had not allowed Mary to enter the library, and seldom went into the room himself, excepting to find something he wanted, or to show the famous hiding-place and the Priest's rooms to some distinguished visitor who could not well be denied.

If the spirit of the old squire appeared to

both the young people before their marriage, it had been remarked that they lived long and happily, and the library was never haunted during their time; but if he only appeared to the bride-elect, she died early, and the library was haunted immediately after her death.

The reader will now return to the two young women above. Spillett opened the door which led to the library and peeped down the stairs. It was quite dark, receiving no light excepting from the open door above. She then lit a candle and, followed by Mary, went down a handsome short winding stairs until they came to a small landing-place below. They looked about but there seemed no door in the wainscotting which surrounded it. The only thing observable was a small bracket in the wall facing them as they descended, which looked as if intended to hold a light.

" I think grandpapa must have had the door taken away, Spillett."

"I do not think so, Miss Mary. We should have heard of the workpeople coming here, and I am sure he isn't capable of doing it himself with all his clock-making; and when the new Dean came here I know they went up to the Priest's rooms, as Mr. Harrison heard them talking about it at luncheon-time, and the Dean said there were some at a place near Guildford he had seen very like them."

"I don't remember it, Spillett; but grandpapa never says a word about the library before me."

" The door is here somewhere, Miss Mary, and we'll find it if we look long enough."

"I wonder if that bracket has anything

to do with it, Spillett? The Italians who altered the house were wonderfully clever in making their hiding-places look natural."

" We'll see, Miss Mary ; " and she caught hold of the candle bracket and proceeded to examine it. Presently she gave it a twist, and a door opened by itself, pressing gently outwards against her.

" We have found it ! " she cried, and she stepped back and let the door open wide. They were now able to enter the closet leading from the library, which has been already mentioned. The door, which had opened upon them, still retained its shelves, which had separated themselves from the others at the corner mitres—the shelves being supported by small brackets.

" We must get through here somewhere, Miss Mary. I expect the other door is at the end," and Spillett proceeded to push and pull at the end of the closet. At length it slid back and then opened, and they found themselves in the library.

Mary thought it very different from what she had expected. She though it would be a larger and finer room. After they had looked about them, Mary went to look for the inscription on the window, an account of which and its importance in the family she had heard from her Aunt Augusta.

"Take care no one sees you from the garden, Miss Mary!"

They peeped cautiously through the window, but there seemed no one about on the quiet Sunday afternoon.

Mary read the lines again and again with wonder, till she almost knew them by heart.

"It's dreadful, Jenny! What does it all mean? I know the heir has always come here before his marriage with his intended bride, and if he does not, something dreadful happens; but I am the heir now, and I shall have to come if I ever marry."

Mary was too alarmed and agitated to study the meaning of the words closely.

Jenny read them carefully, and thought intently for a few moments; she then said, "It isn't so difficult, Miss Mary; I think I understand most of it, and father has told me a little. It means the spirit of the old squire is allowed to escape for a time from his punishment of having to stay here if there is no sorrow in the house, from the master or mistress dying before their time like his own son. It's 'Hand for hand' that nobody can understand, unless it means, as some say, that his handwriting would be known; but I don't think it's that myself, and no one can guess why he appears sometimes to both and at other times only to the bride. I am sure there is something in 'hand for hand' that must be obeyed; if they neither of them come they will both die young, and if they both come and do not do something he wants them to do, the bride will die young — it's awful, Miss Mary!"

"It's terrible, Jenny!" she said, clinging to her tremblingly. "I wish I had never come here."

"No, Miss Mary. You will have to come here, and now you know exactly what it says, you will be better prepared, and I think I shall get to the bottom of it before then, when I have time to turn it

over in my mind; and besides, it's no use
going against things we don't understand
in any case."

"I wonder if poor papa and mamma
came here, Jenny ? '

"That's what no one knows for certain,
Miss Mary. Father says he is almost sure
they did not—the Colonel wouldn't let
them."

"Don't you think it's getting dark,
Spillett ? We had better go."

Spillett was quite willing to leave such
a ghostly place, and they returned to the
closet. But the door in the inside was
closed! For nearly half-an-hour the two
young women used their utmost strength
and ingenuity to get the door open again,
but without success.

"We are caught in a regular trap, Miss
Mary ! We must try and open the other

door." This they found much too strongly
locked to open without proper means.

Mary broke a paper-knife she found on
the table in trying to force back the lock.

" I must climb down from the window,
Miss Mary, and get round. The closed
door will open on the other side."

"Impossible, Spillett! You will never
get through there. A man might, but you
can't, and you will kill yourself in getting
down ! "

" I shall try," said Jenny, and she
attempted to get through, but could not
pass the narrow opening of the old window
and Mary dragged her back again.

" I shall call out, Spillett; we can't stay
here for ever ! "

"Indeed you won't, Miss Mary; I shall
break a way through the ceiling first !
We shall have to wait until they are all

gone to bed, and break the lock off the door with the poker; there is no one at this side of the house at night to hear us."

They then went again into the closet to make another trial, but the fastening of the door defied all their efforts, and they returned to the library and sat down on the leviathan sofa.

" It was very wrong of me to come here, Spillett. I am well punished—and it's getting dark every minute. I think we had better call somebody."

" We must lie down and hide our faces until it is gone, Miss Mary; but now I am here, I don't feel so afraid of it as I did. I will never let you call out till we have tried everything ! "

" Let us go inside the closet again, Spillett, and pull the door to."

Spillett assented most willingly, notwithstanding her vaunted courage, and they started up to go to the closet.

"Bring the light," said Mary; and her maid returned and fetched it off the table. As soon as they were inside, they dragged the outer door again into its place and heard a slight click; they were then going to seat themselves on the floor, when they saw the inner door gently opening itself as before.

"We are saved!" cried Spillett. "Was there ever anything like this old house! I *remember* now hearing father say, long ago when I was a girl, that one of the doors had to be shut to get through the secret passage in the library! It's some spring lockwork, Miss Mary. Father has got a little box that came from Ixstead, when you shut one side the other opens."

They passed through and closed the door; again there was a slight click.

"Do you think that has opened the other door, Miss Mary?"

"No, I don't think so; that has to be moved back first."

"We must risk it, it doesn't much matter. The Colonel will think it's the wind, or the rats, or something, if he happens to come up. I do not think he will come here, as he does not suspect anything."

They returned upstairs. Mary looked very white and sad. She began to think she could never sleep there again another night.

"You must sleep in my bed, Miss Mary, and I shall sleep here. They won't venture inside my room, I know."

"But they might come to the door, and they would know my voice. No, dear

Jenny, you must sleep with me; there is plenty of room for us both."

" Plenty, Miss Mary! it's a famous old bed, and I'll tell you what I have thought of—I mean to make that old white dress of yours exactly like the one in the picture, and then, if you put a red flower in your hair, I'll engage if you meet anybody they won't stop long to speak to you; all you have got to do is to walk like this "—and she imitated a ghostly step she had seen at a theatre—" look hard at them, and pass on quick."

At night, when all was quiet, Mary descended to Spillett's room, but the two friends lay awake for a long time discussing again the writing on the window.

It had made a strong impression on Mary, which deepened on further reflection. Like most of the Doddingsteads, she was highly superstitious. She had been brought up in an atmosphere of ghosts, and her imaginative nature placed an exaggerated importance on their power for good and evil. Healthy girl as she was in other respects, she was nevertheless haunted at times with a dread that she should die young like her father and mother.

She now declared to her astonished friend Jenny, that, even if her grandfather gave his consent, she would not marry Captain Wyldeman unless he passed the ordeal in the library successfully by Richard Doddingstead appearing to both of them; that perhaps her grandfather's instincts were right, and that she was only acting wickedly after all and trying to tempt Providence.

Jenny stoutly combated these new scruples; but as Mary held with tenacity to her resolution, she did not then press the matter any further. She thought that if the Colonel could only be brought to give his consent, love would triumph over the rest.

END OF VOL. II.

PRINTED BY WILLIAM CLOWES AND SONS, LIMITED,
LONDON AND BECCLES.          *S. & H.*